BEAU &
BETT

A Modern Retelling
of Beauty and the Beast

KATHRYN
BERLA

AMBERJACK
PUBLISHING

IDAHO

AMBERJACK
PUBLISHING

IDAHO

Amberjack Publishing
1472 E. Iron Eagle Drive
Eagle, ID 83616
http://amberjackpublishing.com

Book design by Aubrey Khan, Neuwirth & Associates.

Library of Congress Cataloging-in-Publication Data
Names: Berla, Kathryn, 1952- author.
Title: Beau & Bett : a modern retelling of beauty and the beast / by Kathryn Berla.
Other titles: Beau and Bett
Description: Eagle, Idaho : Amberjack Publishing, [2019] | Summary:
"While working off his mother's debt at Bettina Diaz's father's ranch, Beau
LeFrancois is continually surprised and charmed by Bett's frankness,
despite being warned that she's a 'beast'"-- Provided by publisher.
Identifiers: LCCN 2019001002 (print) | LCCN 2019001833 (ebook) | ISBN
9781948705455 (ebook) | ISBN 9781948705448 (pbk. : alk. paper)
Subjects: | CYAC: Conduct of life--Fiction. | Social classes--Fiction. | Dating
(Social customs)--Fiction. | Ranch life--California--Fiction. | California--Fiction.
Classification: LCC PZ7.1.B4578 (ebook) | LCC PZ7.1.B4578 Be 2019 (print) |
DDC [Fic]--dc23
LC record available at https://lccn.loc.gov/2019001002

ISBN 978-1-948705-448

eBook ISBN 978-1-948705-455

10 9 8 7 6 5 4 3 2 1

Dedicated to happiness in all its forms.

May it find you for now, ever after,
and all the moments in between.

ONE

(Once Upon A Time)

For one very long second, I wanted to believe this was someone else's life—anyone who wasn't named Beau LeFrancois. Anyone who wasn't me.

Pause . . . Rewind . . . Play . . .

It'd been a long day at school, which was basically every day and any day. When I walked through the front door, my house was still the tiny, cramped, gloomy box it always was—no magical genie had transformed it into a palace while I was in class. Papa was sprawled out on the sofa like he always was, with one leg, plaster-casted from ankle to hip, resting on the sofa and the other leg slung over the side, foot planted firmly on the ground. Pillows propped behind his back and underneath his broken arm positioned him in a half-sitting, twisted pose that looked uncomfortable, but at least allowed him to watch TV.

"Beau, buddy," he said. "Didn't know if I was going to make it 'til you got home. Help me to the bathroom, would ya?"

"Papa, you can't hold it in all day, it's not healthy. That's what the bottle's for."

"Healthy shmealthy. I'm not peein' in that thing like some kinda animal."

"Animals don't pee in bottles." I shoved aside a pillow and sat my butt down on the couch, taking his healthy arm and pulling it across my shoulders. He still had a strong grip, and his fingers dug into me as he swung that massive cast off the couch where it landed with a hard thud on the floor.

"Garbage dump!" His lips went purple with pain, and the substitute curse words he used—required by my mom—did nothing to mask his frustration and anger at the pathetic situation. "Holy fried apple chicken!" The pain crept up his leg until it enveloped his entire face in a red cloud. "Give me a minute." He took a few jagged, stuttering breaths before regaining his usual composure.

"Did Angie call today?" I asked, hoping mention of my older sister would steer his mind away from the misery of shattered bones.

After a few seconds, his breathing returned to normal. "You betcha," he said, and he was Papa again. We heaved in unison to pull him up into a standing position—a move we were pretty good at after so much practice. "She doin' good but she started in again with that crazy talk about postponin' the wedding. I tole her not a chance. Tole her I'm gonna dance with the bride."

We thumped our way toward the tiny bathroom off the hallway that led to the kitchen—me, the human crutch.

"In five weeks? I don't think so, Papa. Maybe a spin around the dance floor in your wheelchair if you're lucky."

Which of course made me think again about the school dance this past weekend when Masie draped herself all over Ethan the Goose. And why should I care about that? But *why* didn't matter since I did, and I was thinking about it the moment the door burst open and the twins came in, fighting as usual over one of their mindlessly ridiculous and invented catastrophes.

"Poppy, Claude threw my math book in the bushes."

"Did not," Claude said. "Del spit water all over the back of my shirt." He peeled off his backpack, turning to display the wet evidence of Del's crime.

But even before I had a chance to yell at them, or Papa had a chance to empty his bladder, my mom walked through the door as white as a ghost in a snowstorm—not that I've ever seen a snowstorm *or* a ghost. I steered Papa to line him up with the toilet and then gave him a nudge into the bathroom while I waited outside. There was no way he could fall in there with the bathroom being so small and a wall on either side just a few feet away from the throne.

"Charles?" she called out in a voice so shaky I wondered if I was going to have to keep her from falling over, too. "Something terrible has happened."

But Papa couldn't hear her over the urgent stream that wouldn't—couldn't—stop, and his pleasurable moans of release.

"What is it?" I asked, ignoring the twins who by then were bashing each other with pillows from the sofa. "Are you okay?"

Freeze . . . Rewind . . . Stop . . .

Could this be someone else's life? Please?

TWO

My mom sat down on the old wooden rocking chair we inherited after Grandpapa died. She leaned forward and dropped her head into her open palms. Even Claude and Del stopped fighting. Del flew to her side and began to stroke her hair. Claude watched warily from the safe distance of the sofa, wringing his hands in that anxious way of his—waiting for the bomb to drop. By then Papa had shaken, zipped, washed his hands, and was backing out of the bathroom. My heartbeat revved up in a bad way.

"Maman's home," Papa said, totally unaware of the unfolding tragedy. "Come here and give Papa some sugar." Which normally (*yuck*) would've led to the usual *gross!* from Del and sent Claude running out the front door. None of us moved a muscle.

"What's wrong, Maman?" I repeated. And then Papa finally got the idea that something was wrong.

When she looked up, we could see her eyes, red-ringed from crying.

"Maman!" Papa lunged forward, and I had to hold tight to restrain that big old bald Cajun from doing a face-dive in his rush to get to his woman's side. Meanwhile, Del kneeled down at Maman's feet like he was about to propose marriage and took one of her trembling hands into both of his chubby paws.

"It's okay, I'm alright. I'm just a little shaken up. I had a little accident on my way home," she said.

"Are you okay?" we all seemed to ask at the same time—except Claude, who had pulled one of Papa's pillows over his head to muffle any bad news coming his way.

"I was driving home from work and . . . you know that place on Green Valley Road where the avocado grove is?"

I plunked Papa on the sofa where he sat staring at Maman like the rest of us, nobody wanting to say anything that would postpone the rest of the story a second longer. I sat next to him, squeezing Claude into the corner.

"Ya, ya, the Diaz Ranch," Papa said. "I know da place."

"Yes, the Diaz Ranch. Exactly. And as I was driving by, I'm ashamed to say that I saw the limb of one of the trees hanging so far over their fence it was nearly blocking that dirt pathway where people walk or ride their bikes. There was a huge avocado hanging from it where anyone could pick it, and I thought to myself, *Someone's going to take that avocado if I don't.*"

A huge tear slid down her cheek and Del gently wiped it away with the tips of his fingers. "It's okay, Maman." He brought the back of her hand to his lips and planted a tender kiss.

"I know how hard Beau's been working, pitching in around the house and picking up the slack since your accident." Maman was only telling the story to Papa now, like he was the one who ultimately mattered, so why not leave out the middlemen—my brothers and me. "And I thought how nice it would be to make some guacamole tonight since it's Beau's favorite treat."

My heart sank, as if somehow my favorite treat was about to become a reason for this giant calamity.

"And *what*, Maman? Hurry up and tell us da bad part."

"And I stopped the car and put it in reverse to back up to the side of the road where I could get out and pick the avocado . . . which I did. Then I got back in the car and was getting ready to pull out, so I put on my blinker and looked over my shoulder for oncoming traffic. I just didn't see the car coming out of the Diaz Ranch driveway." She looked down at the ground. "And I ran right into it."

"But no one was going fast, right? Nobody got hurt?" I asked more than said.

"Nobody got hurt but a girl got out of the other car, and it was very expensive . . . one of those Range Rovers. I'd hit her front left bumper. She started yelling and screaming at me and told me that I was on their property and look what I'd done. She went on and on, and I've never been so humiliated. I couldn't argue because she was right, and it was my fault and I knew I had the avocado in the car right next to me. She took pictures of my license plate and the front part of her car. She even took a picture of me, as if I was a *criminal*. She asked for my name, address, and phone number and then she told me to move so she could get out."

"Mean-o. I *hate* her," Del said with fury in his eyes. "You shoulda given her a fake name and number."

Wide-eyed, Claude had removed the pillow from his head. "Let's go TP her house, Beau!"

"You two jus' be quiet and mind you'se'f," Papa said. "In fact, go on. Get out. Go play or do your homework. We'll figure it out, don't you worry, Maman."

The twins tried to disappear by moving to a corner of the room. No way were they going to miss out on one second of this excitement.

"It's okay, Maman. At least you're not hurt—that's the important thing, right?" But what I was really thinking was, *Why do all these bad things keep happening to us?* And then Papa answered that unspoken question like he always does whenever something bad happens.

"Some folks got all the luck and some folks don't. We don't got any luck but we got a lot of love so that's all that matters."

So, there you have it. We don't have any luck, the LeFrancois family. But we've got love so that's supposed to make up for all the other stuff.

THREE

"It's not so bad, Hon'," Papa said. "That's why we have insurance. Let me just give them a call right now and they'll take care of ever'thing."

"Charles." By this point Maman looked eerily other-worldly, unnaturally calm like she was talking from a million miles away, and with this glassy stare as if focusing her eyes was something she'd forgotten how to do. If you looked close enough, which I did, you could see her lower lip was trembling. "I . . . I . . . cancelled the policy last month."

Cue the da-da-dum music because I kind of heard it in my head.

"Golly dance!" Papa was rarely shaken but the news kept getting worse, and even his pessimistic view of the Le-Francois family luck was being pushed to the limits. "What a furifying mess!"

"We have to eat, don't we? Angie has to get married. Beau needs new clothes. The twins need to see the dentist.

And you . . ." She dropped her voice to barely audible. "You can't work for God knows how long."

"If God knows, he ain't shared with me," Papa muttered. "I'll be up before you know it. Back at work sooner than . . . ," he trailed off. He couldn't even convince himself, let alone the rest of us. Falling off the ladder while he was picking oranges did more than just physical damage; it made Papa feel for the first time in his life that he wasn't a contributor.

"At least we don't have to repair our car. It still runs okay, right?" I asked hopefully. After all, she'd gotten home somehow, hadn't she?

"I can't let the Ansaris see the damage." Maman was horrified, thinking of the family who employed her as a maid. "They'd think I was an unsafe driver. They'd think the *car* wasn't safe. They wouldn't let me drive Khalil to school in a car like that."

"I could teach you how to drive a stick. Then you could use Papa's truck for a while."

"Beau's got a good idea there." Papa nodded vigorously. "Then when I'm back on my feet we'll have the money to fix your car."

"I couldn't possibly drive the truck. At my age, there's no way I'm going to learn to drive a stick shift overnight. I've tried it before, and it scares me to death."

"How bad is it, Maman?" I stood up and walked to the door with the twins following on my heels. They'd had enough of tragedy by that point and were ready to bounce back the way little kids do. Examining the right front fender of Maman's car would be their next adventure, but I could see the car from the door and didn't bother to go outside. "I could get rid of some of that paint from the other car with rubbing compound." As much as I tried to sound convincing, I knew it wasn't enough. "But I don't think I could do much to make that huge dent disappear."

Papa groaned.

I thought quickly. Khalil went to Castlegate High, the fancy school, while I went to plain old Bridgegate. It didn't take too long to drive from one to the other.

"Khalil has early period, so I can take Papa's truck and drop you off at work and take him to school on my way in. Then I can cut out a few minutes early to make sure I'm there to pick Khalil up when he gets out. Tell the Ansaris your car's getting serviced. The dent guy can come to our house—hopefully we can get him to do it tomorrow—at least to make it presentable, and then you could tell the Ansaris someone hit you in the parking lot or something."

"How we gonna pay?" Papa asked.

"We'll have to cut back on something," Maman said.

"I don't need new clothes." Once again, I thought about Masie at the school dance. Ethan the Goose might look like a tall duck, but his clothes were always nice, and his shoes were always new.

"Angie don't need fancy flowers at her wedding," Papa said. But when Maman looked up at him with those big blues that could always reduce him to a puddle, he lowered his voice and mumbled, "Well, maybe not so many, anyhow."

"So, the big question is—" I started.

"What about the Range Rover?" Maman finished my thought. "I already thought about that. I'm going to the Diaz Ranch tomorrow after work. I'm going to offer to pay in installments. Maybe I can work it off, cleaning or cooking for them on weekends."

"Those people probably got a whole stable of folks like us doing their cooking and cleaning and whatnot," Papa grumbled. This was harder on him than on Maman, I knew that. He was helpless, and Papa wasn't a man who was used to being helpless and standing by idly. Papa was a man of action.

"Maman, you work too hard as it is," I said. "You can't take on another job. I'll go over there tomorrow after I drop off Khalil and talk to them. Maybe they'll let me work it off. When I'm done talking to them, I'll come pick you up. I got this, okay?"

"You see, Hon'? Beau got this under control." I knew how grateful Papa was for me stepping up and taking over for him while he was down. "Now you get your sweet butt over here and give your ole man some sugar, gal."

Then it was my turn to groan, and I stepped outside to join the twins in surveying the damage.

It's nice to have parents who love each other, I thought. *But really? A wrecked car is better than this.*

FOUR

The next morning, Masie was waiting at my locker. Well, not exactly waiting since her locker was right next to mine, but she could've been taking her time, hoping to run into me. Or she could've just been honestly getting her things together with no ulterior motive. I chose to believe the first.

"Hi, Beau," she purred, her voice so sweet and feline. In fact, it wasn't just her voice that was catlike; she reminded me of a kitten in every way, with those green sloping eyes and slinky moves. Even her short blond hair, all soft and spiky. "I saw you out in the parking lot. You drove today?"

I was hoping she'd see me. Normally, I rode my bike because gas was an expense we couldn't afford. In my mind, driving made me seem mature. Ethan the Goose didn't drive; he rode to school with his older sister, who also somewhat resembled a goose in my opinion, although it looked better on her. I thought about the term "gaggle of geese" and imagined Ethan's family all sitting around the dinner table, honking at each other.

"Yup." Why bore her with the details of shuttling a rich kid back and forth to school and then going to the Diaz Ranch to beg for financial forgiveness in the form of a work-exchange program? "Truck," I added pointlessly as if she didn't have eyes.

"We should hang out sometime after school," she said.

Lesson learned. I was much cooler with wheels.

"Sure, yeah, we should definitely do that sometime." I wasn't deliberately playing hard to get. I just didn't know what else to say.

"How about today?"

"Umm . . . oh . . . I . . . uh." *Right. First we'll pick up Khalil and deliver him to his million-dollar mansion where my mom works as a maid. Then we'll go to the Diaz Ranch and see if I can convince them not to call the cops on Maman.*

"Unless you don't want to."

How do girls do this? How do they manage to pull out your guts with just a few meaningless words?

Having loaded up her backpack with books from her locker, she angled her skateboard to fit into the remaining space.

"No . . . I mean, *yes*. I definitely want to."

The corners of her mouth lifted into a smile that revealed sharp little incisor teeth. Along with that button nose of hers, I got an image in my head—one of those white fluffy kittens, a Persian, I think they're called. A Persian cat didn't fit with a goose. It was so wrong. So, so wrong.

"So?"

"I mean, I want to. But I can't."

"Okay, then. If you don't want to."

Realistically, I was too socially ill-equipped to do any-thing but fantasize about Masie. And yet she'd asked me to hang out after school, and being realistic wasn't one of my strong suits. If it happened once, it could happen again, even *if* she'd already walked away with barely a goodbye. But I had a secret weapon. I had the locker right next to hers. For an entire school year. And now I had the truck. Who knew where that might lead?

* * *

Papa tells a story of how he and Maman met in New Or-leans where Maman was visiting relatives. One night, he and his friends were cutting loose on Bourbon Street when he met up with Maman and her cousin Neela. They hit it off right away and talked late into the night. Anyway, that's the PG version, which is thankfully what he sticks to. I'm sure there was some kissing and other stuff that happened, knowing Papa.

"She was this beautiful California surfer girl, and by the end of the night I knew I'd follow her anywhere . . . even to California," he said. "Knew that after five minutes."

"But Maman doesn't surf. She doesn't even like to go to the beach."

"Don't matter. I knew who she was in her heart," he'd say, which never made any sense to me.

But he did follow her to California and they did get mar-ried and have four kids.

"We don't have much luck in the LeFrancois family. But we're lucky in love," was the way that story always ended.

I sure as hell wasn't.

FIVE

"Hey, dude, it's cool you're picking me up but next time pull up closer to the front of school, so the kids can see me driving off with you."

I looked over at Khalil, wondering at first if he was kidding, and then realizing he wasn't.

"In this old piece of shit truck? Are you serious? My mom's car is much nicer."

"Nah, man, it's all good. And you give me more cred . . . no offense to L-Mom."

"*L-Mom?*"

"You know . . . your mom," he mumbled. "Mrs. LeFrancois." He shifted uncomfortably and pulled on the seat belt as if it was choking him.

"L-Mom. That's so weird."

"Hey, well, she practically raised me."

I thought about how sad it would be to be raised by your maid. And I counted my lucky stars I had an actual mom to raise me, when she wasn't busy with Khalil. At least *one* of my parents was mostly there at all times. Khalil's parents were both world-famous doctors and they were never home—traveling to conferences all over the world when they weren't seeing private patients. I stuck my arm out to signal a left turn since the truck had no functioning turn signals.

Sometimes I actually felt sorry for this kid. He was fifteen going on five. He just needed some good old-fashioned attention in my opinion. But it wasn't my job to give it to him.

"Anyway, I'm not going to be picking you up tomorrow, most likely. My mom's car will be serviced by then so it's back to L-Mom, I'm afraid."

"Daaaaamn!" Khalil unsnapped his seat belt and leaned out the window, in the ridiculous stomach-churning, head-turning move some guys do when they see a girl walking down the street minding her own business. "Lookin' good, pretty mama!"

"Put your seat belt back on," I hissed, "or I'll stop the truck right now and get out to buckle you in myself. Then those girls can see what a man you really are."

With our lack of insurance, I didn't need another vehicle mishap.

"Chill . . . chill, brah. Just checking out the fine ladies."

"And why are you talking like that?" I said. "That's not even you."

He groped around for the two ends of the seat belt and snapped it shut. I knew *he* knew I wasn't messing around. I would've stopped the car if I'd had to.

"Just having fun," he said. "You know . . . *fun*. Have you heard of it?"

"Okay, well, just keep in mind that what's fun for you I can one hundred percent guarantee wasn't fun for those girls." I started feeling sorry for him again. In spite of his size, which was bigger than me, he was still just a kid and probably trying to get attention, even if he was going about it all wrong. "I just don't want you to get hurt," I said, this time more softly. "And you really should cool it with the girls. That kind of stuff doesn't work on them."

Listen to me. I had no idea what worked with girls, except now I had an inkling that access to wheels at least might help with Masie. Maybe the Khalil method really did work, but I seriously doubted it. I was all of eighteen months older than Khalil—I was a junior and he was just a freshman—so I felt a certain big brother responsibility, and I'd seen the look on the girls' faces. It didn't look welcoming; it looked more hostile. Why would anyone choose to be talked to that way? Common sense told me they wouldn't, so I wanted to save Khalil from himself.

I glanced at him out of the corner of my eye and wondered if I was being too hard on him. He was a panda bear. Too big to be cuddled but still stirring those feelings in you—as if you wanted to take him on your knee and tell him a bedtime story or something. Just a big old adorable bear. Well, maybe not adorable but . . . endearing somehow.

"How are you liking high school?" I asked. I was already feeling a little guilty about the way I'd jumped on him. I mean, how could you stay mad at a panda bear?

He hesitated just for a second and then I knew he was over it. Khalil was not the grudge-carrying type.

"It sucked the first few weeks when the seniors waited outside the cafeteria and milked us after lunch."

I'd heard about this initiation even though it didn't happen in my school. Our seniors had different methods of torture that didn't involve throwing open milk cartons at unsuspecting freshmen. Thankfully, I survived everything they'd come up with two years earlier when I was a freshman.

"Well, at least you're over the worst of it," I said. "Now you can get on with your life and next year there'll be a whole new crop of kids to take the heat off of you."

"I wish," Khalil said. I noticed the closer we got to his house, the more his language reverted to normal Khalil, which was actually pretty refined with a vocabulary superior to mine. "There's a group of junior girls who torment everyone, but especially the freshmen."

We were on Khalil's street by then, so I slowed way down because there were usually cops patrolling his neighborhood to make sure nobody did anything to make it less of a paradise for the residents. In fact, Maman told me they had their own private security cops—a few patrol cars that never left the area. Which was good for Maman and Khalil but made me a little nervous in case I got pulled over for a busted taillight or something and I had to show proof of insurance.

"Just try to stay low key—under the radar. Don't call attention to yourself in any way," I said, wondering if I was talking about Khalil at school or me driving through that fancy neighborhood.

"Easier said than done," Khalil said. "Those girls only exist to instill feelings of total worthlessness in others. One girl, especially. She has it out for me like you wouldn't believe."

"Dang, Khalil, you're hella smart. Just ignore them, and when you're older, you'll find a nice girl who'll appreciate your . . ."—I flailed around for something a girl would appreciate in Khalil—". . . your mind. Or maybe your wallet." I couldn't resist, but he knew I was kidding around and we were almost friends, so he just reached across the seat and cuffed me with one of those giant paws.

Anyway, who was I to talk? No mind, not like Khalil's. No wallet. No luck.

SIX

I left Khalil at his house happily rooted in his after-school ritual of delicious snacks (prepared by Maman) consumed in front of the TV. In spite of his pleas for me to join him, I knew I had to get to the Diaz Ranch. On my way out, Maman slipped me a few chocolate chip cookies still warm from the oven and gave me a parting hug.

"Bonne chance," she whispered, even though the TV was on too loud for Khalil to hear us and he probably didn't understand French. After all those years of being married to Papa, Maman had picked up a few of his expressions, and we both knew I'd be needing a dose of good luck. "Don't let them hem you in on anything. Don't sign anything. Don't admit any guilt on our part. Just try to appeal to their humanity and ask if they're willing to work something out that would be mutually beneficial to both parties." Maman should've been a lawyer.

★ ★ ★

I didn't have any trouble finding the place; everyone knew the Diaz Ranch, which was a huge spread where they mainly grew avocados. It was about a ten-minute drive from Khalil's house.

Once I got there, I surveyed the scene of the crime. That must be the overhanging branch where Maman stopped to pick the avocado. There was the driveway—really just a long gravel road that went straight back for who knows how long. I could see in my mind exactly how it must have played out. I even thought I could see the bare earth where the Range Rover must have skidded to avoid colliding with Maman's car. But who would be at fault in that case? Couldn't the driver of the Range Rover be just as responsible, if not more, than Maman? I wished that she'd stood up for herself when it all went down. And I hoped the girl wasn't home—the one who yelled at Maman and took her picture.

I turned into the driveway, which was a one-car-only affair, wondering what would happen if two cars were taking this same driveway at the same time, going in opposite directions.

As it turned out, I didn't have to wait long to get the answer to that question. After driving a few hundred yards down the narrow tree-lined lane, along comes the white Range Rover I assumed must be the one my mom hit. And, sure enough, there was the dent in the bumper. And, sure enough, there was a girl about my age behind the wheel.

We both stopped and stared at each other for a fraction of a second before she got out of her car and, looking all mad, took a few steps toward me.

"*One way*," she said, way too loud. Her eyes narrowed to slits and her mouth closed in a tight, firm line. She pointed in the direction she was going just in case there was any doubt in my mind about which way the one way was. She had a thick dark-brown braid that hung over one shoulder, which was about all I could take in without staring. Oh yeah, and she was also wearing a bright yellow dress. Without that cold, flat voice and the way her mouth twisted into a spiteful sneer, she might've actually become the object of my fantasy like most girls did. But the voice took over and kind of drowned out any other impression that could've stuck.

"Back up," she said, as if I were going to challenge her to a game of chicken. It wasn't that her voice was so awful . . . but the feeling behind it was.

I put the truck in reverse and backed up the entire way, with her right on my tail, leaving me absolutely no breathing room at all. Well, not exactly my tail but my hood, which had become my tail. If I'd had to slow down for a pothole or something, she would've rammed right into me. Once I was out on the street about ready to back into oncoming traffic—for all she cared—I pulled into the spot where my mom had probably been when the collision occurred.

At that point, the girl gunned her engine and drove off down the street without even a backward glance, leaving me alone to figure out how to get to the house if that driveway was one-way only. And if it was, why wasn't there a sign? I finally decided to leave the truck on the side of the road and go by foot. Which turned out to be a pretty long walk—maybe a quarter mile since it took me almost ten minutes before I saw the main house, which was . . . awesome. At least I knew *she* was gone, and whoever was home had to be better than her. Or so I hoped.

SEVEN

Did I mention the ranch house was awesome? Sprawling Spanish-style white stucco walls with a red tile roof. Instead of avocado trees, the last twenty yards leading up to the house were lined by palm trees—the short stubby kind, not much taller than me, but with huge green fronds that spilled from the tops like giant toadstools. There was a circular driveway covered by smooth white stones that sparkled in the sun like diamonds. Blood-red geraniums lined the hedges on either side of the massive oak door. And off to one side of the sprawling house were row after row of grapevines, with bright orange poppies filling in the gaps. All this under a sky as blue as my mom's eyes, and maybe even bluer. I couldn't comprehend what it would be like to live in such a place. Khalil's grand mansion seemed like a dump in comparison.

The day was warm and I knew I wasn't looking my best, sweating a bit after the walk, but mainly after the encounter with the girl. I took a deep breath and strode to the door wearing my toughest emotional suit of armor. Lifting the massive door knocker took some effort. It was in the shape of an upside-down horseshoe, maybe made for a horse the size of a tractor. The door knocker made a thunderous sound, suitable for rousing a giant like the one in "Jack and the Beanstalk." I started off with two hefty knocks but after about thirty seconds I threw in a few more for good measure. I wanted the person inside to realize the person outside was not to be messed with.

After a few minutes, and a few more knocks, it was obvious no one was coming. That's when I noticed the tiny white button to the side of the door—the doorbell. I pushed it and heard nothing. Five seconds later, the door swung open.

On the other side of the door stood an older woman, grandmother-aged. She had her hair pulled back in a bun and was wearing an apron. I couldn't tell if she smiled at me or maybe just winced, but she said, "Deliveries in the back."

What? Do I really look that bad?

I thought about the new clothes I wasn't going to be wearing anytime soon because of Maman's accident. I thought about the girl in the Range Rover and how she also must have thought I was a delivery boy when she nearly ran into me in the driveway. I picked up whatever dignity I still had left and straightened my spine.

"I don't have a delivery," I explained. "I'm here to speak to Mr. or Mrs. Diaz."

"I'm Mrs. Diaz," she said and smiled (or winced) again. She was wearing a plain sort of dress under her apron— the type my mom would call a housedress, something she'd wear to work to look presentable but that would also allow her to cook and clean without having to worry about stains. I have to admit, at first I'd taken the old lady for the maid.

"In that case, I'd like to talk to you about the accident my mother had yesterday with your . . ." I hesitated for a brief moment. Here was my chance to get on her good side. "With your *daughter*."

"My daughter?" Her voice crackled. "I don't have a daughter. You must mean my granddaughter." She smile-winced.

"Oh, your granddaughter. I beg your pardon, I mistook you for . . ." I trailed off and let her guess what I mistook her for.

"What's she done now?" The old lady looked impatient. "How much do you want?"

How much did *I* want? Had I just gone from zero to hero? How much could I ask for and get out of there with quickly? But as Papa is so fond of saying, the LeFrancois family isn't lucky—except in love, and love wasn't an issue in this negotiation.

"Who is it, Mother?" A slightly stocky but striking man appeared by her side. He had a sort of rugged look with all straight lines that reminded me of an eagle. We'd gone from grandmother generation to parent generation. The man took one look at me, sizing me up in a flash. "Deliveries in the back," he said.

"He's not here for a delivery," Mrs. Diaz said impatiently, as if speaking to a child. "He's here for something Bettina's done."

My hopes were still high at that point. "I'm here regarding the . . . *accident* yesterday." I hoped that by deepening my voice, I would appear to be older and maybe even a little threatening.

"Oh. You the guy who ran into Bettina's car? I thought she said it was a lady."

Okay, so maybe I wouldn't be getting the settlement I hoped for.

"I . . . uh, I think it's not clear who was at fault exactly. I'm here on behalf of my mom who couldn't make it because she couldn't take time off from work. I was hoping we could reach some sort of agreement."

The old woman moved slightly behind her son before reappearing at his side. She was like a tiny bird—a finch—flitting around and carefully observing me with piercing round black eyes. She nodded her silver head as if to encourage me and root against her absentee granddaughter at the same time. Her son, on the other hand, stared blankly and I couldn't read his expression. "Go on," he said.

"So . . ." I realized I hadn't really thought any of this through beyond Maman's parting instructions that I was scrambling to recall. Something about not admitting guilt. Something about appealing to his humanity.

"Look . . ." I guess he got tired of waiting. "The truth is, your mother was at fault. Bettina took pictures and your mother was evidently on our property. I'm not sure why she was pulled over, but I'm venturing a guess she was after some of our avocados. A lot of people think that's a public pathway, but it's not. That's our property even on the other side of the fence. If you want, I can get nasty about it, but I don't think you want that and I don't either, so I tell you what I'm going to do. I keep a fairly high deductible on collision for our cars . . . a thousand dollars. You pay the deductible and we'll call it even. I'll leave it up to you whether you want to report it to your insurance company or not."

This was a man who was obviously used to giving orders. He gave me a chance to step up, but I hadn't been fast enough. And I knew enough to know that, with a guy like him, once you've had your chance you don't get another one. I'd blown it. A thousand dollars? Might as well be a million. So, we were back to the plan Maman had yesterday. Work it off somehow. But how? And would he go for that? Would he even believe we didn't have more than five hundred in the bank and that was everything we had in the world?

Once again, I struggled to assemble any shreds of dignity still clinging to me.

"Would you accept a trade?" I asked in a voice that threatened to betray my weakness. "I can come around and do odd jobs for you until I pay off the debt."

He stared blankly at me again. The old lady nudged him in the ribs with her elbow. "I'm not so sure Bettina had nothing to do with this," she said.

"Mother, please. Give it a rest and let us work this out man-to-man."

Nice of him to give me at least that much.

"I'll tell you what," he said again. "Even if I could find some work around here for you, and even if I paid you a lot more than I pay my hands, that's still fifty, sixty hours of labor you'd have to give me."

"Yes, sir. I can handle fifty hours. It'd have to be on the weekends 'cause school days I have to help around the house with my two brothers. And help with the chores at home and homework and all. But I could come Saturdays and Sundays until it's paid off. Would that be okay?"

"I'll tell you what . . ." He clearly was fond of telling me what. "You come by this Saturday AM. We get started early around here. You find Ray and report to him. He'll tell you what to do, and God knows what it'll be, but we'll figure something out. We'll say one month. Saturday's the first of the month and when the month's over I'll sign a piece of paper saying we're even. Is that satisfactory to you?"

"Oh yes, that's satisfactory. Thank you. Thank you very much."

The old lady smile-winced and adjusted the waist of her apron.

"I'm a man of means," he went on, just when I thought it was over. "I could pay the thousand dollars with the money this place earns while I'm taking a dump."

My face must have lit up too much with the expectation he was going to let me off the hook.

"But I won't," he said. "And do you know why?"

I shook my head meekly.

"Because I'm goddamned tired of people stealing my avocados. These kids that come around at night thinking they're so smart."

I shook my head to indicate what I hoped was disgust with the kids who were coming around at night, stealing his avocados, thinking they were so smart.

"You're not like that, I can tell."

I shook my head hoping to convey I was nothing like that, while thinking about his daughter who had such a hateful face when she said the words *one way*.

"You're the kind of man who needs to pay off a debt that's rightfully his, so I'm going to give you that opportunity. You'll thank me for it one day."

I couldn't imagine thanking him one day, but I nodded my head to show I would.

He stuck out his hand. "Name's Lupe Diaz, but you can call me Mr. Diaz."

"Thank you, Mr. Diaz," I said. "I'll be here first thing Saturday morning."

EIGHT

The worst had already happened, hadn't it? I was on the downhill part of an uphill climb, so everything should be easier going forward. I knew what was expected from me . . . now I just had to do it. Then why did my breakfast feel like a cold, hard lump in my stomach as I drove to the Diaz Ranch on Saturday for my first day of work?

Turns out we way underestimated the amount of time it would take to fix Maman's car. For one thing, she didn't just have a dent that needed to be banged out—she was leaking oil pretty bad. In fact, there was a complete transfer of oil from her car to our driveway. So that meant more money and more complicated family arrangements. It also meant I had to keep transporting Khalil to and from school. Lucky that was okay with my schedule, timewise. In other words, Khalil spent a lot more time in school than me, and why not? He was destined to be a doctor or lawyer or some other fancy professional. And I was destined for trade school, by choice. That's where my interests lay, so why bother killing myself with unnecessary classes?

Khalil was enjoying my company, a break from his L-Mom. I was older, thereby cooler, in his eyes, but not so old as to be uncool. I also drove a vehicle, even if it was a beat-up truck. Masie had already proven that transportation could make an invisible person like me visible to a girl like her. Khalil didn't drive and there was no reason to believe he'd be driving anytime soon. Most kids by his age are nagging their parents to get at least some hours behind the wheel, but Khalil was perfectly happy being driven by others. When I dropped him off at home that Friday, he asked whether I wanted to come by on the weekend to play video games and maybe shoot some hoops. I guess all that togetherness made him think we were buds by then. He said he had real friends at school but between their busy parents and his busy parents, it was hard to catch a ride. And Khalil wasn't one to walk places.

"I can't," I said. "I have a job that starts tomorrow."

"A job?" It was a new concept to Khalil—something he'd never considered—a kid having a job that would interfere with weekend goofing-off. "Doing what? Babysitting your brothers?"

"Nah, Papa does that on the weekends." *From his permanent seat on the couch*, I didn't add.

"So what kind of job, then?"

I had to be careful. I didn't want Khalil to find out about the accident and tell his parents something about Maman that would cause them to have less confidence in her. Khalil would never purposely sabotage his "L-Mom," but he was so open and trusting he might not think two moves ahead about the consequences of his words. And I couldn't very well ask him to lie by omission.

"Working at the Diaz Ranch. Helping out. Odd jobs."

"The Diaz Ranch!" He yelled so loud I almost drove off the road. "Where Bett the Beast lives? She's one of the girls I was telling you about. Not just *one* of them . . . she's the *worst* one of all."

"Bett the Beast? You mean Bettina? She doesn't look like a beast." I thought about the firm, disapproving line of her lips when she said *one way*.

"Bettina? She goes by Bett at school. And, yeah, she's a beast. Take my advice and stay away from her. She looks okay, I guess, if you dare to look at her."

"Okay, well, I think you're overdoing it a little. She's just a girl—how bad can she be? And anyway, I'm not working for her and I probably won't even see her. I'm working outside on the property."

"Don't say I didn't warn you." He shook his head slowly as if he'd just received some really bad news. "Hey, Beau? How come you never invite me over to your place?"

"We're not really friends, Khalil. I mean, I like you— you're a good dude. But you'd be bored hanging out with me." I paused and took a deep breath. "You wouldn't have fun at my house, trust me."

I looked at him out of the corner of my eye and immediately felt guilty again. I didn't want Khalil to come over and see how we lived. How Maman lived. To see Papa all laid up the way he was—helpless like a baby. Not even able to get to the bathroom by himself.

* * *

So, there I was the next morning, driving to the Ranch, thinking about all the things Khalil had said. Bett the Beast.

What's the worst thing she could do to me? If Papa had managed the transition from alligator-trapper to orange-picker to orange-picker falling off a ladder to invalid on a couch, couldn't I handle a girl my own age? If Maman could work eight to ten hours a day cooking and cleaning for another family before she came home and cooked and cleaned for her own family, couldn't I pick a few avocados with or without a girl looking over my shoulder? If Angie could handle the concept of marriage to an idiot like Jason—who acted like my big brother around my parents and Angie, but picked on me when we were alone—couldn't I man up and breathe the same air as a girl who might have said a couple of mean things to some freshman boys? If Claude and Del could put up with . . . well, the truth is they were just little kids and didn't have to put up with very much except maybe being babysat by me from time to time when I was trying to do homework and had to lay down the law so I could hear myself think.

And by the time all this stuff had made the complete journey through my brain, I'd arrived at the Diaz Ranch. Right where everything started. Guacamole used to be my favorite snack, but I was at the point where I couldn't stand the sight of an avocado. I pulled my truck up as close to the fence as I could and started to park and prepare for the hike down the driveway, until I thought better of it. Mr. Diaz had said this was his property, too. Maybe he didn't want me parking here. Maybe I should try to park in the back where deliveries were made. But how would I get to the back, and why hadn't I asked? Not down this driveway, I knew that much. Obviously, there was another way in, so I pulled the car back on the road, making sure not to replicate Maman's accident. Then I drove slowly down the road until I came to a break in the fence that was pretty much hidden because of the tall oleander hedges on either side. It was the entrance to another long gravel lane that looked like it should lead more or less to where I wanted to go. I signaled a right turn with my arm out the window and crossed my fingers—figuratively, of course.

My tires crunch, crunch, crunched all the way down the lane until I finally caught sight of the house. My instincts had been correct—this lane led to the back, the part I hadn't seen before. There was a big open gravel area with a bunch of cars and trucks parked along the edges. I parked my truck under the shade of a gnarled old oak. I walked past a four-car garage, partially opened to reveal the white Range Rover. A little further on I saw a sign near a narrow door that said "Deliveries." I kept walking, wondering where I could find this Ray person who would tell me what to do. Some men were working in the vineyard, so I decided to start there. Maybe one of them was Ray. Or maybe even Mr. Diaz, himself.

There was a huge fenced-in area between me and the vineyard that looked like a few acres. I walked all the way around, sneaking a peek as I passed. Part green lawn, part fruit orchard, and part jumbo-size swimming pool. The pool was mostly protected from prying eyes by a border of oleander speckled with fuchsia blooms. Fuchsia. Yeah, I know that color, which was Angie's go-to toenail shade. I wasn't completely in the dark about girls, having an older sister and all. Just mostly in the dark.

I decided right then and there to stay away from the fenced-in area. To not get anywhere near the entire massive ranch house and its immediate grounds. It was obvious nothing good was ever going to happen to me over there.

*　*　*

It turns out that working off a debt feels like being picked last for a team. Nobody really wants you, but now that they've got you, they've got to make the best of it. And doing a job that you're not trained for feels like going to a school dance without a girl. You're going to do a lot of standing around while trying to pretend you're part of the scene, but you're really not. So that should give you an idea of what it was like for me that first day.

I eventually found Ray after asking some of the guys who were busy with picking grapes. They pointed here and there, and I wandered up and down a few rows of grapevines before I finally bumped into him. He had perfectly straight posture and long legs that covered a lot of ground with each step. You knew right away he was a guy who had everything under control. His animal spirit, I decided, was one of those Great Dane dogs. Or maybe a Doberman. He was nice enough but didn't have a clue as to who I was or why I was there, so I guess Mr. Diaz hadn't remembered to mention me. But he took it in his stride, said the jefe wasn't around (which I understood was Mr. Diaz), but he'd find something for me to do . . . which turned out to be picking grapes.

Here's how you pick grapes. First off, don't call them grapes, call them berries. Don't ask me why because, to me, a grape and a berry are very different things, but there you have it. Second, you grab a big white bucket and a pair of sharp snipping shears. You probably want to put on a pair of gloves to avoid messing up your hands too much, and then with one hand you hold the bunch of berries and with the other hand you snip the stem at the top of the cluster. Then, when your bucket gets filled, you take it over to this metal container and dump—I mean, gently distribute—the grapes so they're evenly spread out. At some point, the tractor comes by to pick up the full container and leave an empty one. It pretty much goes on like that all day, with you stopping for lunch at a certain point and a few breaks for snacks or water or whatnot. During the breaks you try to find a spot in the shade, but since there weren't very many most of us wound up under one big oak tree together.

One thing all that picking did was give me a better appreciation for what Papa did for a living. Being an orange-picker, he did pretty much the same thing I was doing except he did it on a ladder—which turned out to be a bad thing on the day he got stung in the face by a yellow jacket, which caused him to take a backward dive and eventually landed him on our sofa. He also used a little harness contraption attached to a cloth sack, instead of the bucket I was using. I guessed grape picking might not have been too awful if you had someone to joke around with while you were picking all day, but the rest of the guys were speaking Spanish to each other and I didn't understand any Spanish. If they'd been speaking Cajun French, I could have at least followed along.

During one of our breaks, three or four of the guys were talking and then they all looked over at me and laughed, and I was pretty sure I heard someone say "Bettina."

"What?" I asked. I'd run out of snacks and water by then, so I was sitting a little apart from everyone, contemplating how sore I was going to be the next day when I came back to work. And why hadn't I thought to wear a hat and sunglasses? My nose and cheeks were already feeling more burn than the muscles in my back and shoulders. But at least I was nearly one day closer to fulfilling my part of the bargain.

The men all laughed again so I turned to Ray and raised my eyebrows in a facial gesture I hoped he'd interpret as "what's the big joke?"

"Don't worry about it, kid," he said. "They're just wondering why you're here . . . why Diaz hired you since you're so slow at picking. They figure you must be Bettina's boyfriend."

At the sound of her name, everyone laughed again.

"Oh yeah? Well, you can tell them I'm not. In fact, I don't even know her."

Which I guess he did, which provided one last laugh at my expense before the break was over. So, it was good, I suppose, that I was at least providing everyone with a little entertainment to make their day go by faster. But that day seemed hella long to me.

Just before quitting time, Ray pulled me aside.

"Look, kid, you're not much good at picking grapes. I could keep you busy doing it if it's just a matter of putting in your time 'til you're square with Diaz. But is there something you're actually good at so we don't waste each other's time?"

"Building things," I answered.

NINE

The next morning, I got there early, armed with water, snacks, a hat, and sunglasses. I was really feeling it all over from my labor the day before. When I pulled into the big open parking area, there were no other cars. The garage door was down so I couldn't see inside. With nothing else to do, I turned on the radio, shut my eyes, and waited for everyone else to get there. After a while, when nobody showed up, I looked at my watch and it was already thirty minutes past starting time. I got out of the truck and walked over to the vineyards to see if anyone was there. But after walking up and down the rows of vines, there was no sign of anyone. I knew I'd told Mr. Diaz that I'd be there Saturdays and Sundays, so I wondered why there wasn't someone around to tell me what to do. I hoped I hadn't wasted a trip for nothing. I also hoped I wouldn't only be working Saturdays, which might mean he'd expect me to put up with the Diaz Ranch for two months instead of one.

When I'd given up finding anyone in the vineyard, I walked back toward my truck and saw the narrow door that said "Deliveries." There was a doorbell, so I rang it and then waited for what seemed like a long time. I was just about to leave and go back to my truck when the door swung open, with Bettina on the other side. Her braid was slung over one shoulder the way I remembered it, except kind of messy like she'd either slept in it or maybe just done it up fast. She was wearing a little white sundress, kind of skimpy, but other than that nothing special except it looked good against her dark skin.

"If you have a delivery, just leave it and someone will bring it in later." She started to close the door.

"Wait! I don't have a delivery, that's not why I'm here."

"You're the guy from the driveway, aren't you? The one going the wrong way."

"Yeah, but—"

"Then why don't you have a delivery?"

"I never did have a delivery. I don't even know what you think I'd be delivering."

Her eyes narrowed, and she backed up a little while making a move to close the door like she suddenly realized I was a serial killer or something.

"I'm supposed to be working today," I said urgently, hoping that would stop the door from slamming in my face. "But no one's around. I looked in the vineyard, but I couldn't find Ray."

The door opened a little more and she stared at me. "I thought you had a delivery."

"Well, I don't."

"In that case, I don't know what to tell you. Everyone's at church."

"Oh."

"And they usually don't get back until past noon."

"Nobody told me anything about that."

"So you can come back then."

"I drove all the way out here. Couldn't I just stay and work? Do something until they get back? Otherwise I'd have to go all the way home and then come back again. That's a lot of driving."

"What would you do?"

I looked at her and a strange sensation came over me. I could usually see the animal in a person, but I couldn't get a fix with Bettina. They called her The Beast, so what exactly was a beast? A lion? Crocodile? Gorilla? Something sinister? But she didn't fit any of those. She didn't fit anything at all. She could make a scary face for sure, but when it wasn't directing an angry phrase at me, it didn't seem so bad—in fact, it might even be nice-looking to an outside observer.

"I don't know. I guess I could pick some more grapes. Or maybe you have something else you need me to do. You could tell me what to do."

"You want *me* to tell you what to do?"

She opened the door wide. I had her attention.

"You could. Or I could just pick some grapes, I guess."

She looked deep in thought as if she didn't want to surrender the gift of being able to tell someone what to do. "I think you should clean the pool," she said finally.

"Okay, I can do that."

"And maybe when you're done, you could wash my car." Her eyes lit up.

I couldn't get too mad; after all, I was the one who'd asked her for ideas of what I should do.

"Go around the side gate and I'll meet you at the pool. All the stuff you'll need is in the shed behind the bushes." She disappeared behind the closed door.

I walked along the fence until I found a gate, which I un-latched and closed behind me. There was a path of granite stepping-stones I followed to the fruit tree orchard, which was smothered in such a kaleidoscope of flowers that it made my eyeballs ache to take it all in. There was even a patch of geraniums that smelled like peppermint, gera-niums being one of the few flowers I could actually name since Maman grows them. After that came the lawn, which looked so unnaturally green I had to stoop down to see if it was real grass or that new fake kind. There was a cro-quet course and someone had left out the orange ball near a wicket. There was a little putting green there, too, that looked like it would be hella fun. I kept walking until I came to an opening in the oleander hedge that led to the pool. Right at that opening was a shed that looked more like a dollhouse, where I figured the pool stuff must be. It must have been made for dolls because I had to stoop to go through the door. I flipped the light switch and looked around. It was stocked with just about everything you'd need for a pool and garden: rakes, shovels, long-handled pool nets, bags of fertilizer, croquet mallets and balls, and a few putters and golf balls. I grabbed a pool net, turned off the light, and closed the door behind me.

When I came out on the other side of the hedge, Bettina was already poolside, reclining in a lounge chair with a mug of coffee on the table beside her. She was still wearing the white dress but had added some oversize sunglasses. Her face was tilted toward the sun like she was waiting for it to give her a big kiss. The pool itself looked like blue topaz, without a leaf or blade of grass disturbing its perfection. Not one single insect was in the act of drowning or swimming laps.

"Umm . . . what do you want me to do?"

"Just, you know . . . clean the leaves or whatever," she said with a wave of her hand toward the pool and all the imaginary leaves in it.

"Okay," I said. I began to skim the surface of the water with the net, capturing absolutely nothing in it but going through the motions anyway while she continued to recline, presumably making sure I did a good job.

I dragged that out as long as I could since it was easy work and nice by the pool, even with a net in my hands. I started off on one side, making a few splashing sounds every once in a while like I had just removed something really nasty from the water. I couldn't tell if she was watching me, with those big sunglasses covering most of her face, but I didn't think so since her face was still tilted up. After a while, I moved to the far end and worked there for a while. And when it seemed like I must have had time to clear everything out from that end, there was nothing left to do but go around to the side she was on.

I moved slowly, dragging the net through the water, until I was just at the point where the backs of my legs were only a few feet from her toes. I glanced quickly over my shoulder to see if she'd moved at all. I'd almost been convinced she was sleeping, so I wasn't sure if I was going to have to wake her once I covered the entire perimeter of the pool. She was sitting up with her legs straight out in front of her, dress tucked underneath so as not to show off anything I wasn't supposed to see. I have to admit I was a little scared for a second, the calm and quiet way she was just sitting there, staring without saying a word.

"Why aren't you in church with everyone else?" I asked. Maybe she was like that kid Damien from *The Omen*—not that I was in church myself, but people didn't exactly call me The Beast, either.

"Why should I be?" She pressed her lips together tightly.

"I dunno." I shrugged my shoulders. "Just tryin' to make conversation."

Silence.

Now there really was a bug in the water. Just a little beyond my reach, which allowed me a few minutes of making a big deal of getting it out. Then it was on down the line as I approached the last remaining edge of the pool. I looked at my watch and saw I'd managed to kill forty-five minutes with this nonsense. Not too shabby.

When I was about five feet past the place where she'd been lying, she suddenly stood, walked to the edge of the pool, and flung the contents of her coffee mug into the water. There was a little cloud of brown before it was engulfed by thousands of gallons of chlorinated water and the pool regained its natural sparkle. She sat back down on the lounge chair, primly tucking her dress under her knees.

"Why'd you do that?" I couldn't help myself. It was such an odd thing for her to do; I couldn't allow it to go uncommented on.

"It's good for the water," she said. "It's acid so it lowers the pH and that's better for your skin."

Now I don't know much about science, other than what's on the next chemistry test, but I do know bullshit when I hear it. And I have a stubborn streak that sometimes doesn't know when to quit.

"Do you know how much water is in this pool?" By then I'd given up any pretense of cleaning out imaginary leaves and insects. "And how much coffee was in your cup? Unless you're drinking pure sulfuric acid, that's not going to change the pH of this pool one hundred-millionth of one percent." I wasn't exactly sure about that fraction, but I thought it got my point across.

Her mouth made that tight line and I didn't know if she was about to cry or yell at me. It was hard to tell with those sunglasses hiding her eyes.

"Sulfuric acid?" she said. "That's kind of random, isn't it?"

I started sifting the water with the net again, regretting already that I'd engaged her that way. Nothing good was going to come from that.

"Yeah, it just popped in my head. This dumb song my friends and I used to sing back when we were in . . . like the second grade or something."

"What's the song?"

I stopped sifting the water again. "Just a dumb song. You know . . . a kids' song."

"Sing it to me," she said, just as though she were the Royal Highness and I were the court jester.

"What? No, no way. I'm not going to sing it."

As if Mother Nature herself was conspiring to save me from the jaws of The Beast, a gust of wind blew, and a single leaf landed in the middle of the pool—definitely out of the reach of my net.

"Sing it," she repeated, and this time, without even looking, I imagined she was making her scary face.

I was making a big show of paddling the surface of the water with the net in order to create a current that would bring the leaf close enough to where I could nab it. Why was I so scared of her? She wasn't going to lay a hand on me. What was the worst she could do—fire me? Oh yeah, well, maybe she *could* fire me and then I'd be up Shit Creek. I scooped the leaf and lifted it from the water, and once I hauled it in, I removed it with my thumb and forefinger and carried it over to the oleander hedge where I tossed it.

"Okay, well, if you want to hear the song so bad, I'm not going to ruin your day." I coughed a few times and turned my back to her, so it wouldn't seem so much like I was her performing monkey. Then I sang that old song I hadn't thought about for years.

> Poor old Johnny
> Johnny is no more
> For what he thought was H_2O
> Was H_2SO_4

I chuckled and then went back to sifting the crystal-clear water.

"You think that's funny?" She'd turned around in the chair so her legs were off to one side—the side facing me.

"No . . . I don't think it's funny *now*. But we were what . . . all of eight years old. It was funny *then*."

"But you laughed. I saw you laugh," she said. "Right after you sang it."

"I did not."

"Did too."

Maybe I actually did laugh.

"If I did laugh . . . which I'm not saying I did, but if I did laugh, it's because I felt like a jackass for singing it." *And maybe it's still funny*, I thought. *Poor old Johnny. Haha. What am I, Claude and Del's age?*

"Who's Johnny?"

"Who?"

"Johnny . . . the one who died drinking the acid."

"Holy sh . . . it's just a made-up song about a made-up guy. I'm sorry I even brought it up."

"I was just wondering if it was really about some real boy you wished was dead back then."

"What? No! Oh my God. What is wrong with you?"

I turned to face her but those damn glasses. I couldn't see through them. Her mouth was relaxed at that point, not the tight thin line it'd been earlier on. If I had to guess, I'd say that her mouth wasn't having a bad time at all, but I still couldn't peg her to an animal. And then, just like that, I remembered Johnny Mareno who was in the fourth grade when we were in the second grade and how all of us hated him because he'd steal our money and shove us up against the bathroom wall if we went in there alone. I don't think we actually used the name "Johnny" when we sang that song in the second grade—we'd have been too scared someone might hear us and tell him. We usually used one of our own names, so why was I singing about Johnny all those years later? And how was this girl messing with my head?

"I think the pool is clean now," I said, looking at my watch. It was nine o'clock. At least three more hours to go before someone else took over bossing me around.

She stood up and walked to the edge of the pool, surveying it for a speck of dust, I suppose. "Who are you?" she asked. "And why are you here? Did my father just hire you?"

So, she had no idea why I was there. No idea about my mom and the deal I struck with her dad to pay off the debt.

"I'm Beau LeFrancois. You ran into my mom last week . . . the car accident."

"Oh, her. You mean *she* ran into *me*. The pool looks good, by the way."

"Yeah, whatever. Thanks."

"So why are *you* here?"

With her standing on the edge of the pool like that, I had a brief fantasy of pushing her in and getting that pretty little white sundress all wet.

"I worked out a deal with your dad. I'm paying off the amount of the deductible he has to pay to get your fender fixed."

"I'm not even going to get it fixed. I'm getting a new car next week."

I could feel a slow burn starting in my gut and making its way up through my lungs and throat until it felt like I was one of those cartoon characters with steam coming out of my ears.

"Sucks to be you," I said.

"Why? Why does it suck to be me?"

She stared at me from behind those sunglasses that looked like giant black bumblebee eyes. Maybe that was it. She was a bee—no, a yellow jacket like the one that stung Papa in the face and ultimately landed him in the hospital for a week with a bagful of broken bones. But, nah, that wasn't it. She was no bee. Not even a yellow jacket.

"It's a joke. Obviously, it doesn't suck to be you. You get a dent in your car and then you get a new car the next week."

"They're never the same once they've been in an accident. You can't trust them anymore."

"Oh yeah, is that so? A fender bender is going to make your Range Rover inoperable? I don't think so." *Whoa, Beau, slow down. Shut your mouth before you say something you regret.* "Anyway, congrats. Must be nice. What're you getting?"

"I don't know, Dad hasn't decided yet. But anyway, you can go. I didn't know you were here because of that and I don't want you to work here to pay off some stupid debt my father says you owe."

"Umm . . . I think that's up to your dad. Trust me, I'd love to go if it was up to me. And by the way, it seemed like you thought it was a pretty big deal when it happened. My mom said you hollered at her and took pictures of her and the car. So—"

"I had to do that. Otherwise, my dad would blame me. Who's going to believe a kid over an adult?"

I thought about that one and was pretty sure my parents would believe me over some random adult. But maybe her dad was different, and I didn't want to stir up more trouble than I already had.

"Why wouldn't your dad believe you?" There it was. The Beau who didn't know when to shut up.

"This isn't my first accident. So if it was my fault, he probably wouldn't have gotten me a new car."

I couldn't stand there and listen to the pity party she was throwing herself. "I'm going to put the net back in the shed. Then you can tell me what you want me to do next."

I walked through the space in the oleander hedge that led to the dollhouse shed. I ducked my head as I went in to return the net to the exact spot where I'd found it. Then I ducked back out and almost ran smack into Bettina. She was waiting for me just outside the door.

"Wow, you scared me for a second," I said.

"Why?"

"I didn't expect you to be standing there."

"I thought we were going to find something else for you to do."

"We were but . . . I just didn't expect you to follow me to the shed, that's all. Why do you have to question everything?"

"How am I going to know the answer if I don't ask the question?"

Her giant bee eyes were starting to really creep me out. "Could you please take off your glasses, so I can see who I'm talking to?"

She pushed her glasses up with the tip of one finger and I saw eyes that were softly slanted and . . . kind of pretty. Then she let her glasses fall back down against the bridge of her nose.

"Satisfied?"

TEN

"Okay, what now?" I asked, ignoring her last question. "You said you wanted me to wash your car but if you're going to sell it, why bother? You'll probably just trade it in at the dealer and *they* won't care."

"Let's wash it anyhow. It'll give me time to think up your next job."

"Your decision," I said. "Lead the way."

"Go back the way you came, and I'll go through the house and open the garage door."

I retraced my steps over the lawn, through the orchard, through the gate, across the open parking area, and to the garage. Where I waited. And waited. After about ten minutes, I went and sat on the open tailgate of my truck. After about twenty minutes, I was pretty sure she had no intention of coming out and was just playing a dirty trick on me. Which made me more than a little mad and started a bunch of dark thoughts swirling around my head, like, *If that's the way she wants to play it, I can wait her out.* And,

When her dad gets back, I'll talk to him before she does, so I get credit for my time.

In the middle of all that angry plotting, the garage door rumbled open in slow motion the way they do. First thing I saw was two feet in high-wedge sandals; then a pair of (nice) legs; then some denim shorts; then a close-fitting T-shirt tied in a knot to expose the slightest bit of belly, two arms holding a tray with two glasses; then Bettina's face with no sunglasses but nearly completely covered by a huge floppy hat. She stepped out of the garage, holding the tray carefully so as not to spill, and wobbled over to the truck because of those ridiculous shoes that were totally unsuitable for walking on gravel. I don't know how she could see from under that hat, but somehow she made it without spilling a drop.

"Care for a refreshment?" she asked.

"Thanks." I took one of the glasses, which appeared to contain lemonade. "Why'd you change your clothes?"

"If I have to be out here supervising you, I don't want to get my dress dirty."

I took a big swallow from the glass, and then half-gagged, half-spit it out. "What *is* this?"

"Lemonade," she said innocently. "I spiked yours a little. I assumed you'd be a little more grateful since there's no adult supervision."

"Umm . . . no!"

She glanced down at her shirt. "Look, you spit on me. Good thing I changed out of my dress."

"I . . . you . . ." I sputtered. How was I getting blamed for spitting on her? This girl!

"Fine then, take mine. It's just lemonade." She took the glass from my hand and tossed the contents on the gravel. "I was just trying to be nice."

I couldn't tell if she was really pouting because her face was engulfed in a shadow from the hat, but I didn't want to offend her and cause more trouble for myself.

"I'm not saying you weren't nice." I sniffed the new glass she handed me. It smelled like lemonade. I took a sip and it tasted like lemonade. "I'm just sayin' you have a funny way of showing it." I took a few more sips and it did taste pretty good.

"Here, hold this." She shoved the tray at me with the empty glass. "I'll pull my car out. There's a hose over there." She pointed to a low wall about ten feet away. Behind the wall was the beginning of the avocado grove.

I set the tray and two empty glasses in the bed of my truck and walked over to unroll the hose from its reel. Bettina, meanwhile, backed the Range Rover next to where I was standing and then disappeared into the garage. Then she emerged holding a bucket, some soap, and a sponge.

"I'll sit on your truck so I don't get wet," she said. "Let me know if you need anything."

It was strange the way she wanted to stick around. Maybe she was making sure I wouldn't goof off, but she already said she didn't want me to work. So maybe she was bored. Or lonely. Or just plain weird. When I looked over at her after I'd hosed down the Range Rover and filled the bucket with soapy water, she was lying flat on her back in the bed of my truck—one knee propped up, her floppy hat covering her face.

I attacked the car wash with the same energy I'd used to clean the pool—in other words, at a snail's pace. Bettina didn't seem to care; in fact, once again I wasn't even sure she was awake. And why rush when I still had hours to kill? I took a look at her car. Sure enough, the dent was still there and now that I got a good look at it, I could see it was barely a dent at all. Maman's car had definitely gotten the worse end of that run-in.

I never minded washing a car. It's a relaxing thing to do on a warm day. Usually, you'd get the satisfaction of seeing a car go from dirty to shining clean, which wasn't the case with the Range Rover since it was already clean. But it was mindless work, like everything else around that place, so it gave me a chance to think. I even forgot that Bettina was there for a while.

I started thinking about Masie again and wondering if she really could be interested in someone like me, or if maybe she just had to do something that day after school and needed a ride. She hadn't said anything about hanging out when I saw her at the locker on Friday. She was nice enough, though. Told me she heard Angie was getting married to that "really cute" Jason and asking me all about the wedding, which was basically going to be more or less a glorified family picnic. Papa got some license online that allowed him to perform the ceremony, and then they'd have to go make it legit the next day at City Hall.

Angie was a senior when Masie and I were freshmen—cheerleader, beautiful (or so they say), but none of her popularity rubbed off on me. There were always guys calling her and stopping by the house after school, and I'd have to say it got pretty annoying at times. Then when she had the chance to pick a guy to marry, she picked the biggest loser of them all, a total fake who seemed to fool everyone but me. Luckily, our house was too small to fit them in if they ever fell on hard times. And then I thought about the pullout sofa, and the thought of Angie and Jason moving in with us made me shudder. Jason went through jobs like most people go through underwear, so nothing was ever a hundred percent sure when it came to him. But Masie was still in awe of Angie and always asking about her. So maybe some of Angie's popularity actually did rub off on me—at least when it came to Masie.

A thump came from the back of my truck, interrupting my thoughts. I put everything down and stood on top of that low wall where I could see into the bed of the truck. Bettina's propped-up leg had fallen over and was making a sort of triangle with her other leg. I hopped down and walked over to the truck as quietly as I could to avoid crunching the gravel. I guess you could say she was snoring because I'm pretty sure it qualifies as snoring when a small poof of air escapes from your closed lips at regular intervals, making an audible sound each time. I'd never seen a girl sleeping before except Angie, and she didn't snore. As far as I knew, Maman didn't either—at least I'd never heard Papa complain about it. So, I was a little surprised that girls actually snore, and I got to thinking, well, why *shouldn't* a girl snore? It's something I'd never thought about until that moment.

Then, all of a sudden, Bettina moved her hand to her hat and flung it off her face.

"What are you doing?" she snapped. "Why are you standing there staring at me?"

"I heard something, I'm sorry. I just wanted to make sure you were all right."

Jeez. I didn't want her to think I was some sort of creeper.

She sat up, looking semi-dazed. "Have you finished washing my car?"

I had. I couldn't lie. I'd squeezed about every last second I could from that job. My watch told me it was only ten o'clock so there were still two more hours to go. Two more very long hours.

"I think you'll find it to your satisfaction," I said. "If you'd like to inspect."

She looked at her car from the bed of the truck. "No, I can see it looks fine. So, what should you do next?"

"Pick grapes?" I suggested hopefully.

"Ray would be mad if you did that without him here to supervise. Don't worry, I'll think of something."

She put the hat back on again and hugged her arms around her knees. "Hmm . . . there are breakfast dishes still in the sink. Nana would be happy to see them done by the time she gets home."

"Nah, I'm sorry. I really don't think that's a good idea. I shouldn't go in the house with you and me alone. Nope."

"Why?" She scooted to the edge of the tailgate and hopped out.

All I could think about was Maman and Papa's #1 rule for Angie when she was still living at home: *No. Boys. Over. When. We're. Not. Home. Period.* They never had to worry about telling me the rule about no girls over because I never had any girls over, but I was pretty sure Mr. Diaz would have the same rule and I didn't want to be on the receiving end of his wrath—even if nothing was going on and I was just doing the dishes.

"It wouldn't look right," I said.

She walked right up to me, her face engulfed in the hat-shadow. "Are you worried I'm going to seduce you or something?"

"Ha! No. Ha!"

Was I worried? No girl had ever tried to seduce me yet, and that was sort of the last thing in the world that would worry me if and when it happened. But Bettina? The Beast? Maybe I was a little worried—yeah, maybe I was, if I wanted to be completely honest with myself.

"Then *what*?" she asked.

"Like I said. It just wouldn't look right. I'm the hired help, remember?"

"Whatever."

She walked away and began to pace. I emptied the soapy water out of the bucket and rinsed the sponge and bucket, then squeezed the water from the sponge and set it on top of the wall to dry. I rolled up the hose, all the while looking at her out of the corner of my eye and wondering why she was pacing around like that. Like a caged tiger, which made me wonder if her spirit animal was a tiger, but that wasn't it at all.

"I'm *thinking*," she said like she could hear my thoughts. "About what else you can do since you refuse to do the dishes."

"Again . . . it's not that I'm *refusing*."

"Will you do them, then?"

"Nope."

"Then you're refusing." She began to pace again.

I was wondering how much time we could kill with me watching her pace when she suddenly got an idea in her head and marched over to the low wall where I'd left the sponge and bucket. With an agility I wouldn't have suspected from her, especially in those tall shoes, she grabbed the bucket and leaped over the wall. Then, carrying the bucket a few yards away to where there was a mound of earth that looked to have been dumped by a tractor, she picked up a shovel and started scooping dirt into the bucket.

"Need some help?" I called over to her.

"No, that's alright. I can handle it."

She emptied three, maybe four shovelfuls of dirt into the bucket and then struggled with it back to the wall. At that point I went over the wall and intercepted her—I mean, I couldn't exactly stand there watching her trying to carry that load while wearing those shoes. But she didn't object when I took the bucket from her hands.

"Where do you want this?" I asked.

"Over by my car, please."

I scaled the wall and set the bucket down right next to the Range Rover. She followed me over, using only one hand for support to vault the wall, and I have to say I was impressed. I could see a panther in her graceful but athletic move, but a panther was too nice an animal. That wasn't Bettina.

Once she was by my side, she picked up the bucket, struggling to hold on to it from the bottom where she could gain more control and get a better grip. Then, right before my unbelieving eyes, she dumped the whole bucket of dirt on top of her nice, white, shining car.

"What did you do that for?" To say I was shocked is an understatement. "I just spent almost an hour washing your car, and now look what you've done!"

She put her hands on her hips in a way that must have coincided with a smile on her face, although I couldn't be sure with that hat-shadow.

"Now you can do it again," she announced proudly. "And you can take another hour to do it. Aren't you happy?"

"No," I mumbled. "Not really."

But actually, I was happy once I got over the shock. It was easy work and the prospect of killing another hour outside without doing something even more bizarre was a relief. So I started all over again, rinsing the dirt out of the bucket, stirring up the soapy water, and hosing the loose dirt off the Range Rover. Bettina went back to my truck and sat on the open tailgate, dangling her legs over the side and swinging them back and forth the way little kids do. Neither of us had much to say, but I couldn't lose myself in my thoughts the way I had before, on account of her being wide awake and keeping such a close eye on me the way she was.

After a while, I spoke up just to defuse some of the tension I was feeling. That and the boredom. "So, why *aren't* you in church with the rest of your family?"

"You already asked me that."

"I can't remember what you answered." I kneeled down to scrub the right front rim.

"I said, why should I be?"

"I was just wondering. It seems strange, that's all. Your whole family and everyone being there and you being here."

"Is it strange that your whole family is somewhere else and you're here?"

"That's different."

"Why?"

"'Cause I don't want to be here, no offense or anything."
She didn't say anything for a few minutes and I worried I might have gone too far.

"Well, I don't want you to be here either," she said in the smallest voice I'd heard her use so far. "It's my dad's idea, remember?"

"Anyway," I said. "Let's drop it—none of my business."

"You're right, it isn't," she agreed.

"But don't your mom and dad get mad at you and try to make you go with them?" There was that Beau again. The one who didn't know when to shut up.

"Do you always have to have the last word?" she asked, and I have to admit it kind of threw me when she said that. "Anyway, for your information, it's my dad only. And Nana, if you count her."

"Oh," I said, still thinking about what she'd said about me having the last word and wondering if she was right.

"And, not that it's any of your business," she went on, "but no, my dad doesn't care. It's up to me."

So, that went well.

ELEVEN

I got pretty soaked washing the car for the second time, but the day was warm and getting warmer by the minute, so I didn't mind. What I did mind was having to work with Bettina staring over my shoulder, watching every move I made. I wondered what she was thinking and what she was plotting for me next.

"What are you thinking about?" I blurted out, unable to restrain myself.

She stopped swinging her legs and arched her neck to point her face in my direction. "The same thing everyone else is thinking about."

"But everyone else isn't thinking the same thing. For instance, I'd bet anything that you and I aren't thinking the same thing right now. Or maybe right now we are, but not before I asked you."

"I'll take that bet," she said.

"Well, how could we prove it? We couldn't. Somebody would have to go first and say what they were thinking and then the other person could lie."

"You said you'd bet anything. And now you're backing out."

"It was just a figure of speech. When a person says *I bet anything*, it doesn't really mean they'll bet anything, it just means . . . ah, you know what it means."

"There's some dirt on the right front you didn't get," she said. "Just above the light thing. The headlamp."

"Headlight," I corrected her. "You know what? I bet you're a very literal person. You don't read between the lines much, do you?"

"I'll take that bet," she said without a trace of a smile or humor in her voice. "But how would we prove it?"

"That's just what I'm talking about." I wiped away the tiny speck of dirt she'd brought to my attention. How she'd seen it from that distance, through her hat, I had no idea.

She hopped off the tailgate. "I'm hungry," she announced. "You?"

"I wouldn't say no to a snack."

"Keep working. I'll be right back."

She teetered off on her high-wedge sandals over the gravel parking lot and eventually disappeared out of sight, after going through the side gate that led to the orchard. When she didn't come back after five minutes, I went in the garage and looked around for a towel or a rag to dry off the car. The garage was huge and spotless like everything else around that place—my entire house could've fit inside it. The floors were varnished and shiny, with no oil stains like there were where we parked our cars. At my house, there was no real garage, just the end of our driveway with a tentlike structure that provided some shade in the summer.

There were a couple of cars in the Diaz garage—a Bentley that looked brand new and some tiny sports convertible underneath a tarp I was afraid to lift up. I found a pile of neatly folded rags near the car-washing gear. I grabbed one and went back outside. Still no Bettina and it had been at least ten minutes. But I was already used to her disappearing act and I was almost hoping she'd stay gone this time. Then I'd only have about an hour before her dad was back. I could probably find something to tidy up. Maybe I'd go out front and see if there were any weeds growing around the flower beds.

After about fifteen or twenty minutes, I heard the crunch, crunch of gravel and Bettina reappeared carrying one of the buckets we'd used the day before for picking grapes.

"I brought us some grapes to eat," she said.

"Aren't those wine grapes?" I hadn't eaten any when I was picking them, but Ray had told me they were wine grapes. I had no idea what a wine grape would taste like, but I imagined it might taste like wine. I was also a little hesitant to eat anything they grew on the Diaz Ranch, considering it was Maman filching the avocado that landed me in this mess to begin with.

"They still taste good."

She set the bucket down at my feet and pulled out a cluster of grapes that she slowly dropped into her mouth, tightening her lips to free each individual grape from its stem. When her cheeks were bulging like a chipmunk, she swished the mass of grapes from one side of her mouth to the other and then began spitting out seeds like a machine gun. Then there were a few noisy gulps, after which she spat out a big clump of grape skins.

"Mmm . . ." She licked her lips. "Good."

I'd watched that whole show with my jaw hanging. It was pretty disgusting, really, but I halfway admired her for it and I was intrigued. I picked up a cluster and tried to imitate what I'd seen her do. Somehow things didn't go quite as smoothly for me though. I wasn't quite prepared for the thick skins or the massive number of seeds, or for the way the grapes oozed so much liquid in your mouth all at once. But they tasted pretty good, I'll give them that. Unfortunately, the juice went down my windpipe and I wound up choking on some skins and seeds.

After about two minutes of nonstop coughing, during which time she continued to consume even more clusters of grapes, I finally caught my breath. "I think I'll pass on any more," I said. "But thanks for the . . . snack."

She looked up at me with that maddening flop of her hat covering her eyes, but I was close enough to see her lips and the sticky sweet juice dribbling down her chin.

"I'm going to give you one more chance to do the dishes," she said.

"And I'm going to say no one last time," I answered.

"Okay, well there's only one other choice you have in that case," she said. "Try to beat me in a game of croquet."

TWELVE

I knew it was something I really shouldn't do but I was tired of her overconfidence and bossing me around. I was pretty good at playing games, so how hard could croquet be? This was my chance to put her in her place, with her permission.

We went through the side gate to the path that led through the orchard and back to the huge grassy expanse of lawn. And guess what? The croquet set was all laid out, I assumed the way it was supposed to be because I had no clue. So that's what she was doing all that time. She'd known all along she was going to challenge me to a game and the grapes were probably an afterthought because they happened to be close by.

"Do you know how to play?" she asked.

"No, but it looks straightforward. I'm sure I can figure it out." *This looks like child's play compared to miniature golf*, I was thinking. I was pretty good at miniature golf.

"Okay, because our time is limited, we'll just play with one ball each. This is the starting point. You have to hit your ball through these two wickets and then zigzag over to those, then the two on the opposite side, zigzag back on that side and then back to where we began. First one back to this stake wins. There are some other rules about hitting the other guy's ball and stuff, but I'll fill you in as we go along."

Easy peasy. Now for some payback time. I was excited.

We flipped a coin, which Bettina won, and she started going through those wickets like there was no tomorrow, and I wondered if I was ever going to get a turn. She flipped her mallet around, sometimes sideways, sometimes straight-on, as if it were an appendage. When I finally got my turn, she was already so far ahead I knew I'd have to double down just to catch up. But it turned out not to be so easy to get those wooden balls to do what you wanted them to do on the grass. And then toward the end she slammed my ball with hers and sent it soaring in the opposite direction, and somehow that counted for extra strokes for her. Needless to say, she won and took great pleasure in rubbing it in.

"You weren't very good," she said. "I expected a little more competition."

"Sorry to disappoint," I muttered as I went around collecting the wickets and stakes as she instructed me to do, explaining that the gardener didn't want them in the way when he mowed. "Maybe if I'd played it a thousand times before like you probably have."

"There's nothing worse than a bad loser," she said. "By the way, my dad should be back soon."

Couldn't be soon enough for me.

"Why aren't you off hanging out with your friends today instead of following me around?" *Booyah! Score for Beau.*

"How do you know what my plans are for today?" She gave me a sideways glance. "I might have plans for the afternoon."

"Yeah, well . . . should I put this stuff back in the shed?" I was sweating profusely by then, but she looked as cool as a snowball in an ice storm. In other words, really cold. I didn't wait for an answer because I already knew where everything went. She followed right on my heels and waited for me outside the door like the last time I went in there. At least I knew our time together was almost at an end.

"What school do you go to?" she asked when I came out. "Not mine, or I would have seen you before."

"You're right about that. I don't live in the Castlegate district." Did she actually think I would be there working off a thousand-dollar debt if I lived in a house zoned for Castlegate?

"How do you know I go to CG?"

"Because you live about five minutes away."

"How do you know I don't go to St. Francis or some other private school?"

"I took a wild guess." We were walking through the orchard by then, on our way back to my truck. The flower beds that lined the granite pathway still amazed me. They were an actual visual explosion. A color riot. "And I know somebody who knows you. He goes to CG."

"Who is it? What's his name?" she demanded.

"Just somebody. I don't know that he necessarily wants me saying his name."

"Why not?"

"I don't know why not. Maybe he's shy. Ever thought about that? Some people are shy." I was tired of her always having the upper hand, and this was a mystery I could hold over her that hopefully would drive her nuts.

"That's ridiculous. Anyway, why were you talking about me to this person?"

"We weren't talking about you per se. I just mentioned that I was working here . . . *temporarily*." I added that last word for emphasis. It was the only weapon I had to fight back against the powerlessness I felt in her presence.

"Where do you go to school?" she asked.

"Bridgegate."

"I don't know anyone who goes there."

"No, I didn't figure you would." I latched the gate behind me and she started her crunch-crunch superfast walking across the gravel in her impossibly tall sandals.

"Why not? Why shouldn't I know someone who goes to Bridgegate?"

"I just don't see you as a person who would be hanging out in my town too often, that's all."

She seemed to take that as a challenge. "You don't know that for sure. I might be going there later today. In fact, I am. They have a Target there, don't they?"

"Yeah. If you know it so well, you'd know they did."

"And anyway . . ." She ignored my comment. "I know you, and you go to Bridgegate, so now we're even. We both know someone who goes to the other one's school."

"Uh . . . wrong. I know *two* people who go to your school. You and the other person."

I was wading into the twins' *I'm-better-than-you* territory. I wondered if hanging around two little brothers made me less mature than I was supposed to be at my age.

We heard the sound of a car approaching from the long lane that led to the parking area.

"Uh-oh, Nana's going to bust an artery if she sees the dishes are still in the sink," Bettina said.

She ducked into the garage and disappeared permanently. I figured that was the last I'd be seeing of her that day. I stood by my truck, waiting for Mr. Diaz.

*　*　*

Mr. Diaz pulled up in a long, shiny, black Mercedes sedan. He stopped short of the garage when he saw me standing there. The window slid down and I walked over to the car.

"I didn't expect you for another hour," he said. I could see Nana Diaz in the passenger seat. She was clutching a purse in her tight little hands. "You're early."

"I got here at eight o'clock," I said. "I just assumed. Nobody said anything about half day."

"Eight?" He raised his impressive eyebrows. "What've you been doing since eight?"

Now Nana Diaz was interested as well, and she tilted her ear to make sure she wouldn't miss my answer.

"I've been doing . . . a lot of things. Your daughter—Bettina—" *Idiot! Of course, he knows who his daughter is. Stop acting so guilty.* "Bettina had some chores she wanted done so I cleaned the pool . . . and washed her car . . . really good."

"Ha! Bettina had some chores she wanted done. Is that so?" A big smile spread across his handsome face and he really did seem genuinely amused. But Nana Diaz did not.

"She'd better have the kitchen cleaned up," she said. "If you're going to let her stay home on a Sunday and not do what decent people do, then she'd darn well better do what she's s'posed to do."

I felt a strange pang of empathy for Bettina. I almost felt protective of her. Almost. I just wish I could have lied better to take some of the heat off her. Maybe I should've gone in the house and helped her clean up the kitchen. I thought about the first time I talked to Nana Diaz and she had assumed Bettina did something wrong without even hearing the story. And I thought about how Bettina said she took all the pictures of Maman and the car accident because no one would believe her otherwise. But then I thought about Khalil. And I thought about how Bettina only wanted to be believed so she could get a new car. And I thought about how they called her The Beast at Castlegate High. They must have their reasons for that, beyond the ones I'd seen today. Yup, all that went through my mind in the short space of time it took between what Nana Diaz said and what Mr. Diaz said next.

"I'll tell you what," he said. "I'm sure my daughter worked you hard today so just go home. Consider your workday fulfilled."

For which I was grateful. He pulled into the garage and the door slid shut behind him.

I got in my truck and pulled out carefully, trying not to stir up too much dust that might get on the Range Rover. Then I went around to the front where the circular driveway led to the exit lane. I drove along thinking about what a strange day it had been. Avocado trees to my right. Avocado trees to my left. A blue cloudless sky above me and a free Sunday afternoon ahead of me. I wondered what Papa and Maman were up to. The twins. Angie's wedding was coming up in about a month, and I knew Maman wanted it to be as special as she could make it, given our financial circumstances. Then just as I got to the street, ready to make a left, the Range Rover appeared in a cloud of dust right behind me and skidded to a stop.

I looked in the rearview mirror and there was Bettina wearing her bumblebee sunglasses. I could see the straight tight line of her mouth.

I made a left. She made a right.

THIRTEEN

Monday morning found me at the center of my social scene—my locker. Masie was there but she wasn't smiling much and seemed to have a dark, puffy cloud hanging over her.

"Hey, Beau," she said with no enthusiasm. "How was your weekend?"

"Interesting," I answered. "Yours?"

"Awful. Horrible. Lousy. Etcetera."

"That good, huh? What happened?"

She took a moment to pull out her two remaining books and then slammed her locker shut, with a spin of the dial. Then she turned to face me, her emerald eyes lacking their usual polished gleam. "Ethan and I broke up," she said morosely.

"What? I didn't even know you were together . . . I mean committed. Were you?"

"Yes, of course," she said at the exact moment Ethan walked by with Jolene, a girl I knew was a friend of his older sister, but they looked pretty chummy. Masie dropped her gaze and Ethan didn't even look at her.

"Since when?"

"Since the dance, silly." Masie laughed like that should have been obvious to me.

"But that was just a little over a week ago."

Could people really fall in and out of love in just a week?

"A week. A lifetime." She sighed. "What difference does it make since we're broken up?"

Normally, I would've seen this as a great opportunity to go after the girl of my dreams on the rebound. But she seemed so . . . devastated. Could I compete with the memory of The Goose? Especially since he was still so visible.

"Hey, I'm sorry about that. You were too good for him anyway," I said.

"You really think so, Beau? That's what Krissy said, too."

Krissy being her best friend.

"Yeah, I really think so."

I hate when people asked you to affirm a compliment you've just given them. Like they're trying to milk it for everything it's worth. But this was Masie, so I let it go.

"Well, I'll catch you later," I said. "Better get to class."

"Okay, see you at lunch maybe? And hey, did you drive today?"

That was another big change that happened over the weekend. Maman's car was fixed so I was back to biking it to school. With one catch. Khalil loved having me chauffeur him around and Maman appreciated the extra ninety minutes it freed up to finish her work at the Ansaris so she could go home earlier and work on sewing Angie's wedding dress. So, for the next month, I would take the truck a few times a week to give her a break.

"Not today," I said. "But I'm driving tomorrow."

I thought just that fact was enough to elevate my status. I didn't think about the natural progression of our conversation.

"Cool. You wanna do something after school tomorrow?"

And there it was.

"I . . . uh. I have to pick up a friend from school tomorrow. He doesn't have wheels and he's kind of stuck, so I offered."

"We can go together," she said.

I noticed her nails were painted dark green. Her pinky finger had sparkling diamonds embedded into the nail somehow, although I was pretty sure they weren't real diamonds.

"He doesn't go to school here. He goes to Castlegate."

"All the way to CG just to give someone a ride home? Fan . . . see!" She shook her hand like she was shaking something fancy off her fingertips.

Now, why didn't I just tell her I was helping my mom out, and Khalil's parents were Maman's employers? Most of the kids at Bridgegate were in financial circumstances similar to mine. Most of their parents worked at jobs like Papa's and Maman's. Most of my friends had after-school jobs, although I never did because I had to be there when the twins got home—that is, before Papa's accident. Even so, now I had to be home to help Papa go to the bathroom if he needed to go, although he resorted to using the bottle when I was transporting Khalil.

"Well, he'd do the same for me," I said and realized that probably Khalil would, although we weren't exactly friends.

"Can I come with you? It'd be fun to see how the other half lives." She laughed, giving me a glimpse of those sweet feline incisors. "And besides, I need the distraction," she added with a voice that had suddenly transformed to morose.

How could I refuse Masie?

I didn't.

FOURTEEN

Tuesday morning, Masie told me to wait for her at the truck after school. Unlike me, she had an extra period at the end of the day, so she needed a few minutes to pull off a successful cut.

"It's only PE," she said. "Mrs. Blaylock takes roll when we walk into the locker room. Then when everyone's changing, it's easy to leave without being noticed."

Mission accomplished, we were on our way.

"I think Ethan's together with Jolene," she announced as we pulled out of the parking lot.

"Already?"

I was amazed at the speed with which people fell in and out of love. Only a week ago, Ethan and Masie were officially together, and I had no idea until they were already broken up. Two days later, Ethan was in a new relationship—with an older woman, no less. What did Ethan have that I didn't? It's true he was college-bound, but it was hard to see how that would cause a girl to overlook his annoying personality and gooselike looks.

"That's what everyone is saying."

Everyone didn't talk about me, not that there would've been much to say. Would *everyone* start talking about me, now that Masie and I left school together? And if *everyone* did talk about us, what would they say? Was it possible we were already in love without me even realizing it? Would we be broken up by next week?

"More important is how are you feeling?" I asked.

In my opinion, she should've been feeling pretty great, finally being rid of The Goose and not having spent much time with him in the first place. But I knew that girls liked to be asked how they were feeling. At least Angie did.

"Oh God, I'm up and down. Just when I think I'm over him, I remember something we did together and a whole new wave of grief comes over me and . . ." she trailed off.

I wondered how much time had to go by before she ran out of things to remember that they did together. By my calculation, it couldn't be too long, considering they'd probably only clocked in ten, maybe twenty total hours together. I could put up with her moping over Ethan for another week. Then I hoped, for both our sakes, it would be over.

"Who's this guy we're picking up?" she asked. "How do you know him?"

The moment of truth. No use denying it because Khalil sure wouldn't.

"My mom kind of works for his family," I said. "We've gotten to know each other well." And none of that was a lie.

"Cool."

That was easy.

FIFTEEN

It took about thirty minutes to get to Castlegate, and school was always out by the time I got there. Khalil liked me to pull right up front, which took some time since all the parents and au pairs were there before me. But this was our routine and he knew how long he'd have to wait to make the grand exit he desired. There were still plenty of kids around to see him getting picked up by the "cool" older guy who probably gave off a whiff of danger to the Castlegate students accustomed to Beemers, Mercedes, and Porsches. And that day he was getting a twofer—a hot girl besides. I knew Khalil would be over the moon about that.

When he spotted us, his gentle, giant panda eyes opened wide and he bounded over to the truck. He was decked out in bright red—oversize T-shirt and basketball shorts. I knew Khalil didn't play basketball, except the video game kind.

"That's him?" Masie asked.

She scooted over to the center and fastened her seat belt. We were touching practically everywhere—arms, shoulders, thighs. Five seconds later, Khalil was in the truck, touching all those same places on Masie's other side.

"Khalil, this is my friend Masie," I said, and probably for the first time in his life Khalil was practically speechless.

"Hi," he mumbled, looking straight ahead.

I knew the feeling. He was awestruck by Masie's sexiness. Who wouldn't be? I put the truck in gear and pulled out.

There was a lot of uncomfortable silence in the beginning because I wasn't really comfortable around Masie, and Khalil sure as hell wasn't. Masie herself was probably wondering why she'd cut class to sign up for this. Khalil and I didn't usually have a lot to talk about without throwing Masie into the mix. Add in the fact we were all pressed up against each other like a bag of the red wiggler worms Papa used for composting. But once we cleared the school pickup area, it seemed like everything loosened up and we relaxed enough to be able to communicate on a basic sort of level.

"Your school is nice." Masie was the first to break the ice. "The grounds are a lot prettier than ours."

"Yeah, I guess it's okay," Khalil said, just as I slammed on my brakes to avoid hitting a group of girls who chose to cross right in front of me without even looking.

"Do people around here think they're invincible or something?" I muttered. "They almost got themselves killed."

I hoped this wasn't going to be an opportunity for Khalil to lean out the window and holler out some inappropriate pickup line. But I was fairly confident that Masie's presence would have a civilizing influence on him.

The girls walked at a leisurely pace, chatting among themselves, completely oblivious to us. But then I saw someone I definitely didn't want to see at that moment—Bettina. She stopped for a second, a little island in a moving river of girls, while the others kept going without her. She glared at me and I stared at her as the other girls moved around and away from her. Noticing she was being left behind, she whipped her head around and walked after them. It gave me a strange feeling, seeing her in that group of girls—the way they made room for her, not as The Beast they feared but more as an unwelcome stray. I didn't know what my eyes were telling me. I just knew I didn't like it.

"Oh my God, it's The Beast!" Khalil said in a way too loud voice, especially considering our windows were down. "Beau . . . it's The Beast—the one I was telling you about. Have you started working at the Ranch yet? Have you seen her there?"

"I know, I know," I said, trying to hush him. "I know who she is, okay?"

Then Masie got wind of something big and started up with the questions.

"Who's The Beast?" she asked. "What are you guys talking about? What ranch, Beau?"

I shook my head and made the turn onto the main road. The wind whipped through the hot truck. The top of Masie's spiked hair flattened, giving her a whole different, more approachable look.

"She's a girl at my school and that's what everyone calls her," Khalil said.

"Why? I didn't think she was ugly—she looked okay," Masie said. "She had nice hair." As if nice hair was an important indicator of someone's character.

"No, not because of that. She's just . . . she's mean. She's just plain not nice," Khalil said.

"Like how?" Masie was a hundred percent committed. The ice had instantly melted between Khalil and Masie, and they were bonded in their desire to hear gossip and deliver gossip. I felt like the odd man out. My bare arm was sticky against Masie's. Khalil was wearing a sheen of sweat like a second skin.

"Like once I accidentally bumped into her in the hallway and she said, 'Watch where you're going or the next time I'm going to step on the back of *your* sandal.'"

Masie glanced quickly at me. "Anything else? I mean . . . to be called The Beast?"

"I didn't step on the back of her sandal. Or at least I don't think I did," Khalil said defensively. His brow creased in thought. His eyebrows moved together like they were hatching memories. "Once she told a guy that his jokes were dumb. And another time she threw someone's calculator in the garbage can, or maybe it was hers. And some other stuff."

"I thought you said she made your life miserable," I said. "Other than telling you to watch where you're going, how does she make your life miserable?"

"Every time she walks by the table where I eat lunch with my friends, she makes a nasty face at me. Like this." Khalil did an angry duck face that looked ridiculous on him. It probably didn't look as ridiculous on Bettina and caused Masie to crack up. "And once when I was putting something in my locker, she bumped me really hard and I knocked my forehead against the locker door."

"That's brutal. Did she laugh?" Masie asked.

"She never laughs, or even smiles," Khalil said. "Not that I've ever seen."

"She sounds like a real witch," Masie said, and Khalil nodded in silent agreement.

And all the while I hadn't said a word, but I had this feeling bubbling up inside me that something unjust was taking place and I should do something to make it right.

"I talked to her at work last weekend," I finally said. "And she was okay."

Why was I sticking up for her? The Diaz Ranch was my prison for the next month. In a way, she was my prison warden. Was this a case of Stockholm syndrome, where hostages bond with their captors?

"Okay, you don't know her, Beau, so be careful. Stay as far away from her as you can."

The hot air blowing through the truck's windows alternated between drying my sweat and then kick-starting the sweat cycle again.

"Wait . . . you work for her?" Masie asked. "When did that happen?"

"No, I don't work for her. I'm just doing some hourly stuff on the Ranch. Just part-time, seasonal. You know the Diaz Ranch?"

"That's *her*? That place is huge. She must be really rich. What do you do, Beau? Pick avocados or something?"

"Different things," I said. "Picking grapes, mostly." How could I admit the only other things I'd done were to clean a clean pool and wash a clean car? Oh yeah, and lose at a game of croquet.

"Is that where your dad worked?" she asked. "Is that why you're only working there temporarily until your dad gets better?"

I glanced over at Khalil who was staring at me blankly. How much had Maman told him about Papa's accident? She wouldn't have withheld that information, would she? Did Khalil even think or care about Maman's life beyond what she represented to him—his surrogate mother? Maybe not. Wanting to be careful, just in case, I decided not to go into it.

"No, it's just a job. Short-term."

But I wondered why I was so quick to stick up for Bettina. She was odd for sure, but she'd given me easy jobs to fill the hours she knew I had to fill. Was she doing it out of kindness or boredom or some other unknowable reason? There were a few clues that made me think the first, but plenty of clues that made me wonder about other motivations. I just wasn't ready to let Bettina be thrown to the wolves so the rest of us could have something to talk about. Something to feel superior about. Something to take our minds off our own personal problems. And the hot truck. And the people in the cab of that truck who were so physically close, but in reality were a million miles apart.

SIXTEEN

The rest of the drive to Khalil's house was pretty un-eventful, allowing Khalil to get comfortable enough with Masie to start throwing some compliments her way.

"Your eyes are amazing," he said. "I've never seen eyes that intense shade of green."

Masie lowered her head and cupped a hand under her face. When she looked back up, she was cradling a tiny green contact lens.

"Presto, change-o!" she said. "This is my real color. I'm just wearing tinted lenses."

She stared at Khalil and he sputtered, "Holy shit!"

"Let me see," I said.

Masie turned and stared wide-eyed at me. One eye was that mesmerizing emerald green. The other was goldish with maybe a hint of subtle green tones. I quickly turned my focus back to the road.

"Your real eye color is pretty," I said. "Why do you wear the tinted ones?"

"Just for fun. Same reason I bleach my hair."

"Wait," Khalil said. "Now you're going to tell me you're not really blond?"

"Nope. My hair is probably just a shade lighter than yours."

I tried to envision Masie with hair almost as dark as Khalil's, golden eyes, and that ivory-toned skin color. It seemed even more awesome than the way she looked now. A new fantasy for me to mull over in my darkest hours.

Masie balanced the contact on the tip of her finger and poked it back in her eye. "By the way, where are we going?"

"We're dropping Khalil off," I said before Khalil could muscle his way into our plans.

"No rush," Khalil said. "I have no plans if you guys want to go somewhere. In fact, let's stop off and get something to eat. My treat."

That was exactly what I was hoping to avoid, but Masie turned to me. "Yes, let's, Beau. Can we? Do you have time?"

Well, if I was going to claim I didn't have the time, then I'd have to drop Masie off at her place. If I said I did have the time, then we'd be spending most of it with Khalil. It was one of those lose-lose situations.

"Sure," I said. "But I can't stay too long."

Hedge my losses.

* * *

Khalil wanted to stop at some place that was supposed to look like a funky old diner but in reality was an upscale restaurant with upscale prices posing as a funky old diner. He ordered the works, which meant hamburger, milkshake, and fries, while Masie and I stuck with a Coke. I thought about Maman and how she'd have a snack waiting for Khalil, one that she'd carefully prepared just for him— fresh-baked cookies, spiced cider, something along those lines. I felt guilty thinking about her going to the trouble while we were sitting in the booth talking, laughing, having a good old time. I pulled out my phone and, holding it under the edge of the table, surreptitiously typed out a message letting her know we wouldn't be back for a while and that Khalil didn't need a snack. When I was done, I rejoined the conversation in progress, acting like I'd been listening all along.

"So, then my biology teacher told her to go out and stand in the hall until the message came through." Khalil took an enormous bite from his hamburger, and then used his napkin to mop up the ketchup and meat juices dribbling down his chin.

Masie was cracking up like he'd just said the funniest thing and I joined in even though I had no idea what they were talking about.

"Oh my God, that's hilarious," she said. "He didn't really do that, did he? You're just playing."

"No, for real. I'm telling you exactly the way it went down."

By then, I'd already finished my soda and Masie had finished hers.

"We'd better get going, Khalil. It's getting late."

I thought about Papa at home with the twins, helpless without me or Maman there. I thought about how I finally had some alone time with a girl I'd been fantasizing about since my sophomore year, and I'd just blown it because of

Khalil. Then I looked at my watch and realized the bind I was in. This was one of those days I was supposed to be saving Maman some time, so she could leave early and get things done at home. There was no way I could drive Masie all the way home and then turn around and get back to Khalil's house to pick Maman up without being late. Not even if I took Khalil with us to drop off Masie, which was more than I could bear. Nope, I'd have to take Khalil home and pick up Maman before taking Masie home.

Awkward.

SEVENTEEN

Once Maman got over the shock of seeing a girl in the truck with me, she and Masie took to each other like peanut butter to jelly. Naturally, Maman insisted on sitting in the middle. She wouldn't hear of Masie having to take the "uncomfortable" seat.

"Masie, you and Beau know each other how?"

"We have our lockers next to each other, Maman."

"Plus we had a class together last year," Masie offered helpfully.

"Where did you get this skateboard, Beau?" After bonking her head on it, Maman turned to examine the brilliantly painted board wedged into the narrow space between the bench seat and the rear window of the cab.

"Oh, that's mine, Mrs. LeFrancois. Sorry, I hope it's not in your way."

"Not at all." Maman turned around with renewed interest once she learned it belonged to Masie. "That's a beautiful design."

"Thank you! I painted it myself—sort of a hobby of mine."

"And you ride this thing, too? Or you just paint them?"

"Both." Masie laughed, flashing her fascinating pearly whites.

But after that it was more or less smooth sailing once Maman got used to the idea of (A) a girl in my truck, and (B) a girl who rides skateboards. Everything else was a piece of cake, even with Maman being a barrier between me and Masie.

"Did you all have a good time at the diner? That was nice of Khalil to treat you," Maman said. "Will you still be hungry for a big dinner, Beau?"

I froze a little because I'd tried so hard to text Maman on the down-low without drawing attention to myself. I didn't want Masie to think I was a kid who needed to report his every move to Mommy. But then I thought about it for a second. I didn't mention Khalil treating us in the text. And I didn't think I'd mentioned a diner either.

"How did you know?" A risky move since Maman could come right back at me and say *From your text, of course.*

"Khalil texted me. Right after you picked him up."

A bittersweet moment because I was no longer under suspicion of being the guy who reported to Mommy. On the other hand, was Khalil a better son than me? He'd provided more details and texted much earlier. But wait. That sneak! He had it all figured out as soon as he laid eyes on Masie—he planned the whole thing of stopping off at the diner, not exactly a spur-of-the-moment decision like he made it seem. Khalil was smooth, I'll give him that.

"Awww . . . that's so cute. He's so sweet to text you and let you know where we were." Masie said it like she really meant it, and I think she did. Which, of course, made my mom like her even more. What mom could resist a girl who wanted the boy she was with to report back their every move? I couldn't even win at being a mama's boy.

"Mrs. LeFrancois, I'll bet you're really excited about Angie's wedding."

This girl knew how to pick topics near and dear to Maman's heart.

"We're all really excited, aren't we, Beau?"

To which I nodded to demonstrate my excitement, even though I wasn't generally a fan of weddings, and specifically a fan of my sister's fiancé.

"If you need anyone to do calligraphy, I'm really good at it," Masie said. "I can do place cards since you've probably already done the invitations."

"It's very informal," Maman said. "We're trying to keep the budget low and it's just going to be family. But place cards," she said dreamily. This was an unexpected touch of class she hadn't considered. "Place cards would be delightful if you wouldn't mind."

"I'd love it!" Masie said. "I need to practice my calligraphy more and I don't get many opportunities to show it off. I'm pretty artistic so I can help in other ways if you need someone to draw anything. Or help with flower arrangements."

"I'm afraid the only way I could pay you back is with an invitation to the wedding," Maman said. "We have to cut back on flowers because her wedding cake is so expensive. And we decided to pay for a professional photographer even though Beau offered to do that."

"I offered . . ." I said, ". . . to do that."

This was getting out of hand. Masie was being usurped by Maman before I even had a chance to win her over with my natural charms. And what if things didn't work out the way I hoped they would? Four weeks was an eternity as I'd come to find out. We could fall in love and break up two or three times before Angie's wedding.

"No, you definitely want a professional photographer," Masie agreed. "That's one thing you don't want to scrimp on. I mean . . . we're talking about lasting memories to share with your grandchildren."

Who would've thought this sassy and sexy yet tough skater girl would be pondering grandchildren? We were still just grandchildren ourselves. What alternate universe had I just landed in?

"My feelings exactly," Maman said.

This conversation was taking a depressing turn: Maman and Masie semiofficially aligned against me and my pathetic attempt to play a role at the wedding that I didn't really want in the first place. I had only offered to take pictures to be nice, but now it seemed vitally important that I should be the photographer. Dang, Khalil and his diner!

Without even thinking about what I was doing, I drove straight to Masie's house, and it wasn't until I pulled into her driveway that I realized I should have asked her for directions and pretended I had no idea where she lived. Now, she'd think I'd been Student Directory stalking her, which I had been. It wasn't far from my house, but there was no good reason I should know where she lived. We had no common friends.

"Oh, wow. I'm already home. Thanks for the ride, Beau." If any red flags were raised in her mind, she at least didn't let on. "Why don't I come by your place sometime after school this week, Beau, and we can get started on the place cards?"

We? Place cards? Papa. Del. Claude.

"Sure," I answered weakly.

"What days do you have to pick up Khalil?"

"He's free Thursday after school," Maman generously offered. "Do you have our address?"

"No, why don't you give it to me."

Which she did.

"Bye, sweetie," were Maman's parting words.

Sweetie?

EIGHTEEN

Thursday afternoon came around with nothing much to disprove Papa's often repeated theory about the Le-Francois family being unlucky in life but lucky in love. I wasn't exactly lucky in love yet, but Masie's expected appearance at any moment was at least trending in the right direction, even if it was just to work on place cards for the wedding.

But looming over everything was the single image I couldn't shake: Bettina's fierce gaze when I was driving out of the Castlegate parking lot a couple of days earlier. It was just like in the movies, where two eyes meet across a crowded room and time stands still while the rest of the world carries on. But this wasn't one of those moments in a love story where the girls in the audience are going *aww*, and if the boys are being totally honest, they'd admit they were doing the same thing, only keeping quiet about it. Instead, this was one of those moments in a horror movie where the guy is shaving and he looks in the bathroom mirror to catch the reflection of a killer holding a knife that is just about to plunge between his shoulder blades.

So, yeah. Bettina. In another forty hours, I'd be heading back into the lair of The Beast. But first, the place cards.

* * *

Masie showed up, skateboard under her arm, wearing a knit beanie and black, chunky-framed glasses instead of her contacts.

"I can see better with my glasses when I'm doing calligraphy," she announced, addressing my surprised look.

I had full view of her true golden eyes, somewhat amplified behind the lenses of her glasses. With the dark beanie covering most of her short hair, I got an inkling of her natural beauty, which was substantial.

If Papa could've thrown himself off the sofa to greet her, he would have. Everyone was so obviously excited a girl had come to visit me, it was humiliating. Even Claude and Del opted to stay inside, in order to observe us. Maman had left a list of the wedding guests and set up a card table in the living room where Masie could work and where Papa could more easily embarrass me. There was no real role for me, but that didn't stop Maman from setting two seats at the table. I took the spare seat, mainly to prevent Claude or Del from sitting there and getting on Masie's nerves even more than they already were.

Papa kept up a steady commentary, while Masie focused on the card in front of her, holding her pen as carefully as if it were a stick of dynamite. While she wrote, the tip of her tongue peeked out from between her lips, but when she'd pause to examine her work, she'd bite her bottom lip in concentration.

"You go to school with my boy?"

"Yes, Mr. LeFrancois." Masie's eyes never left the card in front of her.

"Bzzz, bzzz, bzzz."

"What's that you sayin', Del?"

"He said Beau has a girlfriend!"

"I did not."

"Did so."

"You young pups get over here and sit with your Poppy."

Shuffle, shuffle. Del and Claude moved to Papa's side for about thirty seconds before slinking back to where Del could look over Masie's shoulder while Claude crouched at her feet underneath the table.

"You got any brothers or sisters?" Papa could never let a silent space go unfilled.

"I have an older brother, Mr. LeFrancois. He's a year younger than Angie."

"You know my Angie?"

"Sure, everyone knew who she was at school."

"She's a beautiful girl, my Angie. Smart, too."

"Papa, let Masie concentrate. It's really hard to do calligraphy."

"Shoor, shoor. You go on ahead. Don't bother with me."

"It's no bother, Mr. LeFrancois. I like your accent."

"That there's a Cajun accent. That's our people from *my* side of the family."

"He's from Louisiana," I added, since most people in California had no idea what Cajun was.

"Tha's right. Tha's right."

"What heritage is Mrs. LeFrancois?" Masie asked while keeping her eyes glued to the card she was working on.

"California surfer girl," I said, which prompted a roar of laughter from Papa.

"California surfer girl, tha's right."

"Papa, shhh," I said.

And on it went pretty much like that until, after a couple of hours—and an aching back from the uncomfortable chair—we finally had our place cards along with a waste-basket half-filled with unsuccessful attempts.

"Oh no! I forgot to make a card for you, Beau."

"That's okay, you've done enough."

My feelings were only slightly hurt.

*　*　*

By then Maman was home and over the moon about the place cards. She asked Masie to stay for dinner, but she had to get home. The only real time we spent one-on-one that day was the ten-minute drive when I took her back to her house.

"It was really nice of you to do the place cards," I said. I wondered if I was supposed to lean in for the kiss before she got out of the truck. I mean . . . I knew that's what you angled for after a date, but this wasn't exactly a date and it didn't feel right. And if there were signals I was supposed to pick up on before getting the green light to move forward, I was pretty sure she wasn't transmitting any.

"No problem, really, Beau. In fact, it was good because it kept my mind off Ethan. I didn't think about him more than twice the entire time I was at your house. It was fun, too."

"Glad it helped," I said, trying my best to disguise the disappointment in my voice.

"Your family's really sweet, and so are you. See you tomorrow."

"See you tomorrow," I said.

I was wrong. She *was* transmitting signals. Just not the ones I was hoping for.

NINETEEN

I blew through Friday night even though one of my friends had a party at his house. Granted, there were only six guys at said party and all we did was sit around and play video games, but that would normally be sufficient to heighten my mood at the end of the school week. That night, though, all I could think about was waking up early and reporting for work at the Diaz Ranch the next day. And Bettina—would she be there? Hopefully, she'd leave me alone since I'd be working with Ray and the other guys. But why did she give me that killer-stare the day I picked up Khalil? Was she mad at seeing me somewhere I didn't belong? Would she make me pay for it somehow? Khalil told me to "stay as far away from her as you can." Sometimes I had my doubts about him, but he was smart and had firsthand experience with Bettina's anger.

I was one of the first to arrive Saturday morning, so I pulled my car into the shady spot under the big oak tree. I figured I'd head over to the vineyard where I could see a few people already at work. One of the garage doors was fully open, so naturally I took a look to see if the Range Rover was there. I was hoping not to see it and I didn't, even though the garage was full of cars. There was the Bentley. There was the tiny convertible, still covered with a tarp. There was the black Mercedes sedan. And there was a big, bright, shiny red truck. Brand new. No license plates. Double cab. Enough horsepower to pull my house around town. But no sign of the Range Rover, so I guessed I wasn't in danger of running into Bettina, at least not right then.

Over in the vineyard I found Ray and Carlos, one of the other guys I'd worked with the previous weekend. Carlos was trimming while Ray unloaded buckets from the tractor that was parked between where the vineyard met the avocado grove.

"Beau," Ray called out when he saw me. "You're back. Wasn't sure we were ever going to see you again."

"Why's that?" I asked somewhat hopefully. I didn't think I had any choice but to come back.

"Just messin' with ya, buddy." He laughed. "Diaz told me you came last Sunday, and Bettina put you to work."

Carlos chuckled at the sound of Bettina's name, but he didn't say anything.

"Yeah, well . . . at least I got in my hours."

"That you did," Ray said. "And then some, if you ask me. Should've probably counted for double. But enough of that, the question is, what're we going to do to keep you busy today?"

"Pick grapes?" I suggested.

"That didn't work out so well last time if I remember correctly," he said. "I'm not sayin' you did a bad job, but you filled one bucket for every four the other guys picked. Last time I asked what you were good at and you said—"

"—building stuff." I finished his sentence.

"And what kind of . . . *stuff* . . . would that be?"

"Anything. I like to work with my hands. I want to be a builder—get my contractor's license one day. I'm pretty handy."

"Well, I think I have just the project for you, in that case. You game?"

I shrugged my shoulders. "I'm here to do whatever you tell me to do."

"We've had a few near misses with rattlesnakes lately. It's the time of year they're thinking about going back to their dens and settling in for the season, so they're on the move."

"O . . . kay."

What horror did Ray have planned for me? Was this something Bettina somehow finagled? Payback for whatever I did wrong the other day? Not giving her enough competition in croquet? Not doing the dishes when she asked? Showing up at her school where I didn't belong? Existing?

"Well, needless to say, Diaz doesn't want them showing up poolside when he has friends over for a barbecue, or find one tangled up in the pool filter like last year."

My stomach clenched at the idea of a rattlesnake tangled up in a pool filter. That concept didn't resemble any reality I'd ever entertained.

"And we sure don't want Bettina to trip across a six-footer while she's out there pounding the croquet balls around the course or practicing her putting skills, do we?" He snickered.

"I don't know about *her*, but personally I wouldn't care for it," I said.

Was he still messing with me? It was hard to tell with Ray. I thought about the shed and the orchard and how there hadn't been any thought in my mind about rattlesnake encounters. Sure, I lived in California and knew they existed—but I lived in the city where we never saw them.

"Although the babies are much worse than the big ones." Ray was still talking about rattlers. "They may be tiny and sound like a bumblebee instead of that frying bacon sound the big guys make, but they don't know how to measure themselves so they release all their venom at once. But you know this already, right? I'm just boring you."

"Yeah, sure I know."

I wasn't bored, but I felt sure he was trying to get a rise out of me, so I played it cool.

"*Serpiente cascabel*." Carlos grinned. He made a rattling sound by vibrating the tip of his tongue against the back of his teeth.

So, it was *tease-Beau* day again. Glad they were enjoying themselves at my expense, although I did notice Ray and Carlos both wore thick denim pants tucked into sturdy leather boots in spite of the warming sun.

"Alright, so I get it. What do you want me to do today?"

TWENTY

Ray walked me over to the fenced-in part of the Diaz Ranch, the part that separated their personal living space from the rest of the Ranch. This included the pool, grassy lawn, and small orchard. I'd been in and out of the side gate a few times already, so I was familiar with it. What distinguished this fence from the fence that surrounded the publicly visible part of the ranch was that this one was made from metal bars spaced about four to five inches apart. Very decorative but sturdy. It was meant to keep out deer, coyotes, and bobcats.

"We're going to build a snake fence around this entire perimeter," Ray said.

But apparently it wasn't meant to keep out snakes.

"It should also have the added benefit of discouraging skunks and raccoons."

Or skunks and raccoons.

"How do we do that?" I asked. I'd never heard of a snake fence.

"We'll trench the entire perimeter right up against the fence. We'll go down about eighteen inches and then sink some sturdy mesh before filling up the trench. The mesh will extend about yay high." Ray leaned over and put his hand at about a level of two or three feet above ground. "You'll have to tack it to the fence to keep it in place. Think you can handle it?"

"Yeah, sure." It seemed easy enough although it looked to be an awesome amount of work considering the size of the property. "Where are the tools?"

"Follow me," he said.

*　*　*

Lucky that Ray provided work gloves because I could already feel blisters sprouting even with them. Without gloves, my hands would've been raw meat after ten minutes. I could also tell my shoulders and arms were going to be crazy sore by the end of the day. Not to mention the backbreaking part of the job. The good part—I got to work on my own with nobody looking over my shoulder. Luckily, I'd remembered to bring hat, shades, and music source. I plugged in the earbuds and was ready to roll. Ray told me he wanted me to do all the trenching first, but to begin he wanted to see a stretch of the completed job on all of the yardage leading up to the side gate—maybe about twenty yards or so. He wanted to see the entire thing including the mesh fencing sunk, buried, and tacked. He needed to make sure I was doing it right before giving me the go-ahead.

The work was monotonous, but there was a certain satisfaction each time I cinched one of the plastic ties, securing the mesh to the fence, and cut off the end of the tie with shears. I was making progress. Inch by inch. Foot by foot. And, finally, yard by yard. *Try to get through this fence,* serpiente cascabel! I thought of Carlos's imitation of the rattling sound and a shiver passed up my spine. Was Bettina's spirit animal a rattler? I played around with that idea for a bit before finally rejecting it. She didn't look anything like a snake. Her scary face that I'd first seen that time in the driveway when she said *one way*—I hadn't seen much of it since then. Maybe I was overthinking the whole Bettina thing. And why was I even thinking about her when I could instead be focusing on my job, and the tunes, and Masie's pretty face framed by those big chunky glasses—and the way she poked her tongue out while she concentrated on her work.

A shadow fell over me, and for a second, I was confused about the weather. It'd been nothing but blue skies and sunshine when I started work that morning. I looked up at the sky and then whipped my head around. I pulled the earbuds out, my heart pounding.

"You scared me," I said to Bettina, who stood behind me wearing really tight white jeans, a silky royal blue blouse, and another pair of high-wedge sandals. She had on a big, broad-brimmed white straw hat and a different pair of oversize sunglasses. Her hair hung loose.

"Why do I always scare you?"

"Because you creeped up behind me. I didn't know anyone was there."

"On the contrary. I did not creep, I made a lot of noise. I even said hello."

"Well, I had my earbuds in, so I didn't hear you over the music." My heart rate was back to normal, but a feeling of unease had settled in.

"That's not my fault," she said. "I did everything I could to make my presence known."

"I never said it was your fault." I sat on the ground and leaned up against the fence. I guessed it would be okay to rest a few minutes. I'd already accomplished a lot.

"But when you said I scared you, it sounded accusatory."

"Well, it wasn't accusatory. I was making a simple statement, that's all."

"Okay, I accept your apology."

With her standing there, she blocked out the sun, so I pushed my glasses up off my face and wiped away the sweat from my forehead with the back of my hand.

"It wasn't an apology," I said. *Shut up, Beau. Just cut your losses and let this girl be on her way.* But I couldn't. Why did Bettina get to me the way she did? "It was just a statement of fact."

"Well, I choose to give you the benefit of the doubt and accept it as an apology."

"Whatever," I said.

"You have dirt on your face," she said. "Where you just wiped."

I started to wipe away the spot where I'd just wiped before realizing it wasn't going to help.

"Now you have more," she stated.

"That's the least of my concerns," I said. "I'd honestly better get back to work before your dad or Ray comes over and chews me out for slacking off."

"Dad just left and Ray's working in the vineyard."

"In any case, I'd better get back to work because I want to finish up to the gate before Ray comes over to inspect."

"But there's something I wanted to tell you," she insisted, and I knew I wasn't going to get anything done until she had her say.

"Okay . . . what is it?"

"Actually, three things."

"Number one." I stood up and brushed the dirt off the back of my pants. With her tall sandals, she was the same height as me and we stood eye to eye. Or sunglasses to shades.

"Do you like my hat?"

"It's okay," I said. "It's fine, I guess. *That's* number one?" I couldn't care less about her stupid hat.

"Guess where I got it."

"Umm . . . I have no idea."

"Guess."

"Hawaii."

"No, I mean guess what store."

So where does a girl like her shop? I remembered Angie talking about Neiman Marcus for her wedding dress, but saying it was way too expensive. Maman was making all the dresses now.

"Neiman Marcus."

"Nope. I got it at Target," she announced just as proudly as Del would show us an A+ on his spelling test.

"Congratulations." *What does she want—a Brownie button?*

"Remember? I told you I was going there last week."

"Mmm-hmm. Okay, back to work!"

I picked up the trenching shovel I'd been using and plunged it into the ground.

"Number two," she said really loud.

"I can hear you," I said. Even though I'd put the earbuds back in, I didn't have the music turned on.

"It seems as if you're listening to your music."

"It's not on." I deposited a shovelful of earth to the side and plunged again.

"Number two. I talked to my dad last week and told him I didn't want you to work here anymore. That it wasn't your fault and I could pay for the deductible with my own money."

"And?" She had my interest. I leaned the shovel against the fence and turned to face her again.

"And he said that my money is really just his money and besides, you need to learn responsibility."

"I know responsibility."

"And I said that, too. But he said you seemed like someone with character and you'd be offended if he didn't carry through with the bargain. That it would be a good life lesson for you."

"I wouldn't be offended," I mumbled.

"I didn't think you would either," she said. "But once Dad gets something into his head, it's hard to talk him out of it."

She removed the hat from her head and smoothed the side of her hair before replacing it. Her hair was shiny and silky, all loose like that under the sun. I retrieved the shovel from its resting place and plunged once again.

"Now comes the good part," she said. The other two parts hadn't been so good, so I guessed anything else had to be better.

"Is that number three?"

"Did you see my new car?"

"Nope."

By then I'd dug enough to lay down a whole row of wire mesh. I walked back to the place where I'd left off and she followed, I suppose waiting for my undivided attention before sharing number three.

"It's in the garage," she said. "I left the door open this morning so you could see it."

I had to think for a second. "I looked in your garage and I saw your regular cars. Plus a truck."

"That's it!" It was the first real smile I'd ever seen on her face and it looked pretty good. At least better than what was usually there. "That's my new car."

"The new truck is your new car?"

"Yeah, do you like it?"

"Well, yeah, I mean I like it a lot. But I'm kind of surprised *you'd* want it."

I walked along the length of trench that I'd dug and unrolled the mesh.

"Do you think you could grab that other end and lower it into the hole when I tell you?" I asked. "It's kind of hard to do that part with just one person."

As quick as a squirrel, she scampered over to pick up the other end of the mesh roll.

"Okay, one . . . two . . . three . . . set it down."

Once it was positioned in the trench, I started filling in the hole with earth.

"I thought you'd like it," she said. "The kids at school thought it was ridiculous, but I knew you'd appreciate it."

"Why'd you get a truck?"

"I liked just being able to lie in the back of yours last week. I could read in there. Maybe even set up a chair. It's just like yours."

"Your truck and my truck are nothing alike," I assured her. "For one thing, there's about a twenty-year age difference. For another, there's about a sixty-thousand-dollar price difference. Why'd you get such a powerful truck if that's what you wanted? Why not a Tacoma or something smaller?"

"Dad said if I got tired of it, he could use it for the ranch."

"It's going to be a massive gas hog."

"I don't drive very much."

From the sound of her voice, I could tell her smile was gone. I guess I'd killed her buzz. I turned around and could see the familiar downward tilt of her mouth.

"You don't like it," she said.

"I told you I like it. What's not to like? It's just . . . it's just an unusual choice, that's all." Why couldn't I just say I liked it and be done with it? Be done with her? "I like it," I said. "I really really like it. You're a lucky girl, and I mean that."

The barest hint—a memory—of that short-lived smile returned, and something ached inside of me. She turned around and walked back toward the house.

TWENTY-ONE

What goes around comes around so maybe I deserved it. The pride I had in a job well done, even if it was forced labor. The soothing tunes of my music. The warm day and the satisfaction of working out my muscles. All of that was gone in a blink just because I didn't register the right amount of satisfaction over Bettina's truck. And her hat. And maybe I should've jumped up and down with joy because she tried to convince her father to release me from the deal. And was I supposed to commend him for insisting on building my character? Whatever. It just felt like a lousy job again—which it was, so why bother pretending otherwise?

I hadn't reached the gate yet when Ray came by to see how I was coming along.

"You did good, Beau. Nice job. Go ahead and finish up to the gate, then you can trench the rest."

Fifteen minutes earlier, that praise might have lifted my mood, but now I couldn't shake the gloom. Ray left to go back to the vineyard and I went back to my monotonous pattern of digging, dropping the mesh, filling the hole, and cinching the ties.

When I was within five yards of the gate, Bettina reappeared, and the sky darkened again. She'd done another complete wardrobe change, which I now understood was her usual pattern. This time she was wearing tight, ripped, faded jeans; high-top pink Converse sneakers with a picture of that white cat with the big head and a red ribbon in its ear; and a white T-shirt that looked a lot more expensive than the ones I wore, sleeves rolled up almost to her shoulders like a 1950s hipster. Her hair was in double braids and she wore a pink baseball cap with that same white cat that was on her shoes. She had huge hoop earrings that almost touched her shoulders. And, of course, oversize sunglasses—a different pair.

"Hello," she said as though greeting me for the first time that day.

"Hi," I responded. "What's up?"

"I brought you a snack," she said, producing an energy bar from her back pocket that I thought would've been too tightly fitted to her to contain an energy bar.

"Thanks." I ate it in about two bites and then looked around for a place to set the wrapper.

"I'll take it." She shoved the empty wrapper into the same back pocket. "I thought I'd help out. You said it went much faster with two people lowering the wire mesh into the hole."

So, this was her work outfit?

"The only thing is . . . once I get to the gate, I'm supposed to just trench the rest of the perimeter. Ray doesn't want me laying down the mesh until I'm done with that."

"Oh."

"So, while I really appreciate your offer of assistance . . . I'm afraid it won't be necessary." And then I quickly added, "But thanks for the offer. And also the energy bar."

I went back to what I was doing, but she didn't leave.

"Who was that in the truck with you?" she finally asked.

I'd been waiting all morning for that question. Or at least something like it.

"That was my friend," I said. "The one I told you about who goes to Castlegate."

"The girl?"

"No, the boy. His name is Khalil."

"I've bumped into him at school before," she said, and I had to choke back a response to that literal statement.

"Who was the girl—your girlfriend?"

I basically had the liberty to answer this any way I wanted. After all, she'd never find out the truth. Did I want to be the guy with the hot girlfriend? I could *be* that guy, at least in Bettina's eyes. She'd never know. Did I want to answer noncommittally and leave her wondering? I could do that, too. The cool guy. I could be anything or anyone I wanted at that moment. Well, almost anyone since my financial circumstances were obvious to her. Not to mention the LeFrancois bad luck. But in the end, I went for the truth. Because I was *that* guy and I was no good at being anyone else.

"Just another friend," I said.

That seemed to satisfy her.

"If you don't need my help, do you want my company?"

She had a straightforward way of talking, and when someone has a straightforward way of talking and asks you a question, it makes it hard to do anything but give them a straightforward answer. And if that means answering in a way that makes that person feel lousy, well, it's not such an easy thing to do.

"Sure," I said, trying my best not to sound more excited than I actually was.

TWENTY-TWO

She plunked down on the ground next to me, chin resting on knees, arms wrapped around her legs. Her big hoop earrings splayed out against her shoulders. "Why were you there that day—at Castlegate? Just picking up your friend to hang out after school?"

"Something like that." *Plunge. Scoop. Discard earth. Plunge. Scoop. Discard earth.* "Actually, my mom's car was getting fixed on account of the accident with you." *Plunge.* "And it's her job to pick up that kid—Khalil—from school, so I took over." *Scoop.* "And then she wanted me to keep it up a few days a week, so she can get home from work earlier and work on my sister's wedding." *Discard earth. Wipe sweat from brow.*

"Oh, so that kid—Khalil—he's not really your friend, then."

"Technically. Why?"

"Just wondering. Because he's annoying, that's all."

I'd reached the gate with my last roll of wire mesh to lay down before continuing on with the trenching.

"You wanna help out?" I asked, and Bettina jumped up, eager to help. "Grab the other end and hold it in place . . . just a little overlapping with the last roll . . . about two inches. Okay, one, two, three, lower."

I began shoveling the discarded earth back into the trench.

"I don't think he's annoying at all," I said, even though I sometimes did. "And, he actually is my friend. Technically, that is."

"What's a technical friend and how does that differ from an actual friend?"

"What's so annoying about him?" I ignored her question.

Bettina sat down on one of the granite stepping-stones. "Well, for one thing, he was walking behind me down the hall between classes one day, and he stepped on the back of my sandal. So, I tripped and dropped all my books."

I stomped back and forth along the re-earthed trench to pack it down tight with my shoes.

"I can do that if you want," Bettina offered.

"Nah, that's okay. Anyway, stuff like that happens all the time in school. I'm sure Khalil wasn't trying to do it on purpose."

"Maybe, maybe not," she said. "Anyway, he didn't apologize or offer to help me pick up my books, which I consider to be extremely rude."

"Did you say anything to him? Maybe he didn't even realize he did it."

"Oh, he realized," she said. "He and his friends were just . . . *whoops* . . . *haha*. Did I mention the strap of my sandal broke and I had to walk around with it all day?"

"No, you didn't mention that."

I sat on the ground to cinch the ties, so we were actually sitting pretty close at that point.

"Well it did. And I did."

"Did you ever let him know you were upset about it?" I asked. "I'm just wondering because there's a possibility he doesn't have a clue you're mad at him for that. I'm just sayin' . . . some people, mainly guys, are clueless about social cues and all."

"Social cues, ha!" I looked at her and that scary face was back for just a second, or was it my imagination? She pulled her sunglasses up just enough to let me see her eyes narrow into tiny slits that could be reminiscent of a snake, although I'd never actually looked a snake in the eyes before. And her mouth tightened into a straight line. "And yes, I did let him know how it felt. I'm quite sure he picked up on my social cues." She shoved her glasses back down.

"Sorry I brought it up," I muttered in a way that wasn't convincingly sorry.

I worked in silence for the next few minutes.

"Was that girl technically your friend or actually your friend?"

"The one who was sitting next to me in the truck?" I asked as if there were any other girls anywhere else in my life, in the truck, out of the truck, or you name it.

"Yes, that one."

"She's an *actual* friend," I said and felt happy I could say it and have it be true.

"Does that mean that you're *actually* in love with her?"

To say I was surprised at that question is an understatement. But she didn't ask it in a mean way, which I would've ignored.

"No, it doesn't mean that."

But was I?

"What's her name?"

"Her name is . . . Masie." I pulled the cinch tight and snipped off the end with the cutting shears. "How about you? Who's the lucky guy in Bettina's life?"

"You know, that's the first time you've ever said my name." Her mouth relaxed into something close to a smile. She removed her cap and I had an almost uncontrollable urge to pick one of the many spectacular flowers within an arm's reach and tuck it behind her ear.

"What? No, I'm sure I must have said your name before."

"Nope. Not to me."

"Are you sure?"

"Positive."

"Well I know your name, obviously. It's very pretty. I heard your dad say it . . . your nana . . . Ray. Maybe Khalil said it, too."

"Him, too? Khalil? Why—were you guys talking about me?"

Maybe not a wise decision to have included Khalil in that list.

"That's okay," she said. "I know he hates me. Everyone at school does. My nickname's Bett but everyone calls me The Beast at CG."

"That's crazy," I said. "And I don't even believe it. Everyone couldn't hate you at your school. I saw you walking with a group of girls, so you obviously have friends."

"They're my technical friends but not my actual friends," she said. "I don't have any actual friends—not since last year."

"Why would you say that?"

"Because it's true."

I cinched the very last tie leading up to the gate. I was done and, judging by my watch, it was time for lunch. I was hot. I was tired. I was ready for a break.

"What happened last year?" I sat on the earthed-in trench and leaned back against the snake fence.

"They turned me into a beast," she said.

"Why'd they do that?"

"I dunno," she said, and I'm not sure if it was the kitty cat shoes or the hat or the braids in her hair but she looked like a sad little girl just at that moment. "Maybe because they think I am."

TWENTY-THREE

Bettina stood up.

"Isn't it time for your lunch break?" she asked.

"Yep, I was just about to do that."

"Where are you going?"

"I guess I'll just go eat in my truck."

And then she disappeared in that maddening way she had of appearing and disappearing without warning.

Before I could leave, Ray came by to check on things. "How do you like the work?" he asked, apparently satisfied with what I'd done.

"It's fine," I said. "I have the hang of it so it's starting to go faster."

"I need to move some of my guys to the avocado grove this afternoon," he said. "If you feel like doing something different, we could try you out there picking. You game?"

I was fairly certain Bettina wouldn't follow me to the avocado grove, so I'd have the advantage of being alone. And I was tempted to say *yes*, I really was. But was it actually such an advantage to be alone? Might it not get a little dull out there in the grove, just me and the avocados—my next closest human neighbor probably too far away to talk, and possibly not at all interested in talking to me? What was the music policy in the grove? Were earbuds that blocked out all incoming voice commands acceptable?

"My dad busted his hip and leg and collarbone falling off a ladder picking oranges," I said. "He's pretty much housebound right now. Couch-bound, in fact. He's basically an invalid."

Ray drew in a sharp breath and let out a slow whistle. "Well, okay, I'm glad you brought *that* up. We'll keep you away from ladders while you're working here."

"No problem, your decision," I said, although if I was honest, it was the decision I'd been angling for. "I'll do whatever you need me to do."

"Go on and take your lunch break. See you back here in an hour."

TWENTY-FOUR

I walked back to my truck, all the while doing a mental calculation of how much time I had left to go before me and the Diaz Ranch had seen the last of each other. I needed to work a total of four full days, four half days. I'd done a half day and, counting today, one-and-a-half full days. That left me with two-and-a-half fulls and three halves. I started to calculate all that in my head using algebra when my thoughts headed off in a different direction. It wasn't so bad at the Diaz Ranch and there was a positive side, which was missing all the wedding prep going on at my house during weekends. Angie had dress fittings and Jason usually came along with her. If I was home, I'd be expected to seem interested in all that fretting about table settings and flowers. Or at the very least I'd have to talk to Jason and maybe get on the wrong end of his verbal barbs. I decided the Diaz Ranch was as good a place as any to wait out the pre-wedding weeks. As good a place as any, where I had no say in the matter.

I got to the gravel lot and was looking forward to a quiet lunch break. Maybe listen to some music while I ate the sandwich Maman made that morning. Maybe take a look at that new graphic novel a friend had loaned me last week. But when I saw my truck, I could see Bettina's brand-new truck parked right alongside it. And not only that but her tailgate was down, and there was a small white plastic table and two molded chairs set up in the bed. Bettina was sitting in one of the chairs and she waved me over. I by-passed my truck and went over to hers.

"I hope you don't mind that I parked so close," she said. "You were hogging all the shade."

"Oh, no problem. I was . . . just coming to get my lunch. I was going to . . . take it over . . . there." I pointed vaguely behind me.

"You said you were eating lunch in your truck."

"I'd been thinking about it, yeah. But then I thought it being such a nice day and all I should maybe just take full advantage, you know?"

"But I planned a surprise," she said, ". . . for you."

It wasn't until that moment I took the time to observe everything on the table. There were real china plates with potato salad and fried chicken and slices of fruit in a bowl in the center. Real silver forks and knives and spoons. White cloth napkins. Real glasses filled with something that looked like iced tea, and hopefully wasn't spiked with vodka like the lemonade had been. And Bettina—she was wearing a short dark-blue dress with white butterflies. Her hair was loose and brushed out, and she wasn't even wearing a hat or sunglasses. I never realized until that moment she wore practically no makeup like some of the other girls, at least not that I could tell. And that she looked pretty amazing if I had to be honest.

"You're kidding, right?" Most people might not have had that reaction to such a nice *surprise*, but the whole thing was so damn overwhelming and inappropriate. "Do you know what your dad would do if he came out and saw us having a little tea party in your brand-new truck? His darling daughter and the guy he doesn't even know who's working off a debt. Do you know what Ray and the guys would say? I'd never hear the end of it. They already tease me and say I'm your boyfriend 'cause they can't figure out why the hell I'm even working here. They'd skewer me. I'd be dead meat. Toast. Done for. Ruined."

But with each new declaration of what I'd be if Ray and the guys saw me, the corners of her mouth drooped a little more and I thought I saw her chin kind of tremble.

"It's not a tea party," she said. "It's just lunch."

Her voice was so small, which made me feel like a villain. I knew in her strange alternate universe, she was making a nice gesture. All I was trying to do was allow her to see it through the lens of reality. And I wasn't succeeding.

"It's too much." I was exasperated. "*You're* too much. We don't even know each other. We're not even friends, technical or actual. I'm a worker, get it? I'm here because I'm forced to be here."

Oh, how did I ever manage to work up the nerve to say those things to her? How did I harden myself to flatten another human being like that? I might as well have run over her with my truck that day at Castlegate High.

And still her face remained expressionless—at least for any outsider to see. Only I could see. Only I was close enough to witness the trembling chin and lips tightened against her emotions.

We stood there like that, me outside the truck looking up at her sitting just like the Queen of England in that fancy little getup she threw together while I was talking to Ray back at the gate. Or maybe she didn't just throw it together. Maybe she had it planned all along.

"Ray and Carlos and Eduardo think you're my boyfriend?" she finally asked, breaking the heavy silence. After everything I'd just unloaded, I couldn't believe that was the best she could come up with.

"And the others, too," I said.

"All of them?"

"I think so," I said. "I don't speak Spanish, so I can't say for sure."

"None of them ever said that to me."

"Why would they? You're the boss's daughter. And you're a girl besides. Guys will say stuff around other guys they'd never say around a girl."

And then we were back to silently staring at each other but, strangely, that ridiculous interlude somehow defused a lot of the tension.

"My dad's gone," she said, at last breaking our newest silence. "And Nana went with him. They went into town, so they won't be back for a few hours."

I looked behind me toward where the vineyard was—the last place I'd seen the crew working. I didn't hear or see the tractor. Probably they were all in the avocado grove resting in the shade and eating their own lunches. I put a hand on the lowered tailgate and hopped into the back of her new truck.

"Have a seat," Bettina said, her face suddenly as bright as the sun.

I sat.

TWENTY-FIVE

Bettina picked up one of the white cloth napkins and arranged it on her lap, so I did the same. Then she lifted her glass and tilted it toward me as if she was toasting. She took a few small sips before setting it down.

"It's half lemonade and half iced tea," she said.

"Arnold Palmer."

"Who's Arnold Palmer?"

"The drink is an Arnold Palmer. I don't know why it's called that or who he is . . . I guess the guy who invented the drink was named Arnold Palmer."

"Here's to Arnold Palmer." She lifted her glass, tilted it in a toast, and took another sip. "An amazing drink inventor."

But I'd been working in the sun all morning and I was ravenously thirsty. Or maybe it's supposed to be ravenously hungry, but I was the equivalent of that when it came to thirst. I gulped my entire Arnold Palmer without stopping for a breath. Then I let out a big "Aaah" and set the empty glass on the table.

Bettina raised her eyebrows and fixed her gaze on me; without looking away, she lifted her glass to her mouth and downed the entire contents in about two seconds. Then, oh so delicately, she patted her lips dry with a corner of her napkin and belched so loudly I almost jumped out of my seat.

"Okay, that just happened," I said.

"Try the fried chicken," she said. "It's very good."

"So . . . is this actual fried chicken I can eat with my hands, or—"

"Technical fried chicken?" She finished my thought. "You can eat it any way you like."

"Okay, I just wanted to make sure since everything is so fancy and all." The fried chicken did look delicious and I picked up a drumstick with my hands and started gnawing on it, probably looking somewhat like a caveman.

Bettina watched me for a few seconds before picking up her knife and fork and carefully carving the chicken on her plate. She speared a tiny piece with the tip of her fork as though she were about to feed a miniature-size baby. She chewed delicately, looking around here and there but not looking directly at me. She speared a minuscule bite of potato salad and set to work on that. After a few minutes of this, I dropped the remainder of the drumstick on my plate and reached for the napkin on my lap. I wiped down my fingers and all the grease around my mouth, then picked up my own fork and knife.

"I'm not going to eat with my hands if you're going to eat like that," I said.

"Why shouldn't you?"

"I dunno. Kind of takes all the fun out of it."

"I didn't think about that," she said as though she would think about it now.

Then she reached into the bowl of fruit with her bare hands and started pulling out various bits of the fruit salad and popping them in her mouth—orange, grape, apple, banana. When her mouth was full, she began to talk to me.

"Help yourself to some bread," she said as she uncovered a basket of bread that had been hidden under another white napkin. Except she was talking with her mouth so full it sounded more like, "Hph yphsph t'suh brd."

"You're weird," I said. "Really weird."

She chewed and swallowed and chewed and swallowed and finally her mouth was empty again.

"Why do you say that? I was just trying to encourage you to be comfortable enough to eat any way you like."

She dabbed her mouth delicately with her napkin.

"Okay, I can appreciate that. In fact, I *thank* you for that. But I think I'll just use my utensils since you went to all this trouble."

Truth was, I really wanted to eat the chicken with my hands, but I was determined not to let her think I was uncivilized.

"But do you really think so?" she asked.

"Think what?"

"That I'm weird."

By then I had a mouthful of potato salad, and I wasn't about to match her in the talking-with-your-mouth-full department, so I worked on chewing and swallowing until everything was on its way down to my belly.

"It's not that you're weird, you're just different," I said.

A hornet landed on the chicken and she swatted it away with her bare hand.

"Different how?"

I didn't want to spoil her lunch, but she asked like she really wanted to know.

"Everyone is different but you're different in a different way."

"Wouldn't everyone be different in a different way . . . by definition?"

We'd both stopped eating by that point, which was too bad because I was still hungry and, honestly, the food was amazing.

"It's just that you have no filter," I said. "I'm not saying it's bad different. I'm just saying it's different, that's all."

"What's the point of a filter? I don't see the point of having one."

"Well, with a filter . . . You don't have to say everything you think, you know."

"If I don't say what I think, how will anyone know what I'm thinking?"

She pulled the napkin from her lap and set it on the table, which I took to mean she was done eating. She scooted her chair back a few inches from the table, which I took as absolute confirmation she was done eating.

"Look," I said. "If everyone just walked around saying exactly what they were thinking, there would be all kinds of fights breaking out all over the place. There would be world wars. Societies would descend into chaos, and it could be the end of civilization."

She stood up from her chair and glared at me, her eyes narrowed, and her mouth straightened into that scary face.

It was then I realized it had been me who started the whole confrontation, and there I was practically blaming her for bringing on the apocalypse.

"You can say what's on your mind," I said meekly. She was still glaring at me through those angry slits. "But maybe you don't always have to be completely . . . honest?"

The last word came out like a peace-offering type of question, but then again maybe it was me having the last word just like she said that one time.

"Does that mean I shouldn't believe anything you tell me?"

"No, of course not. I didn't mean that, but you . . . but I . . ."

I was hopelessly overmatched.

She sat down and scooted her chair back to the table. Her eyes relaxed and widened a bit. Then a bit more.

"Dessert?" she asked.

TWENTY-SIX

I have to hand it to her, it was one of the tastiest lunches I'd had in a long while. But when my hour was almost up, I was nervous Ray would come around looking for me, and my life on the Ranch would pretty much be over if he caught me in the back of her truck like that.

I started making a stack of all the dirty dishes and utensils. "Look, I'm sorry I can't help you take all this inside and wash up, but I think you know how I feel about going in your house. I'll carry it to that delivery door. How's that?"

"That's fine."

I laid everything on the tailgate and hopped off the back of the truck. Then when she came to the edge, I held out my hand to help her down the way any guy would offer to help a girl about to make a three-foot jump while wearing a short dress and high sandals. But she ignored my hand, kicked off her shoes, and jumped, landing on the gravel with bare feet.

"That couldn't have felt very good," I said.

I could see from the wince on her face that it didn't, but she wasn't about to let on.

"My feet are really tough," she said, which I didn't believe, although I knew for a fact that *she* was.

She slammed the tailgate shut. "I'll come get the table and chairs later," she said.

"I think I'll take care of that for you as soon as I put these dishes down. Where do they go?" Leaving behind the evidence of two chairs and a table was an invitation for someone to start asking questions about the scene of the crime, if you could call it that—which I did.

"In that storage area against the back wall of the garage."

"And if you don't mind, could you take care of those dishes soon? I mean, I don't want to sound like your nana but there's two of everything unless you normally use multiple plates and glasses."

"Relax, I'll take care of it. It's not like we *did* anything. You act like I just seduced you or something."

That was the second time she said that and, it's true, it's not like she seduced me. All we'd been doing was talking, or mostly arguing. I was just a little jumpy about the whole thing.

"Hey, look, it was nice of you to do this, but I don't think we should make a habit out of it, if you know what I mean."

"I'm not in the habit of serving lunch to people, so don't worry."

We were standing in front of the delivery door and I'd just handed her the stack of dishes, so I didn't want to hold her up any longer. I also wanted to hurry and clear out the table and chairs before my hour was up.

"I'm sorry about today . . . the things I said. Some of it might not have come across so nice, and I didn't mean it that way. I appreciate the effort you went to."

She looked at me but didn't say anything.

"What are you doing for the rest of the day? Any fun plans?" I was fishing for an answer that would prove there weren't hard feelings between us.

But she stepped through the door and closed it behind her, disappearing inside the house without so much as a goodbye.

TWENTY-SEVEN

The rest of the day I was out there all by myself, inching my way along the perimeter of the fence at a snail's pace—a sleepwalking snail. I began to wonder if I'd made the right decision and if maybe I should've taken Ray up on his offer to pick avocados. It couldn't have been any more tedious than my current job—or any more lonesome.

I tried to conjure up an image of Masie to distract me and I blasted the music to levels guaranteed to give me permanent hearing damage. But every time I thought about Masie, Bettina's face would float into my daydream like a black cloud covering up the sun until it was just Bettina's face, and I couldn't even visualize Masie. When I did manage to focus on Masie, it was hard to know if she was the green-eyed, blond-haired Masie or the golden-eyed, brunette Masie. The entire afternoon I kept expecting a shadow to fall over me, which would turn out to be Bettina standing there in that unannounced and strange way she had of showing up out of the blue.

But Bettina didn't come. No shadow. No Bettina. And why couldn't I stop thinking about her, anyway? Must have been the guilt I was holding on to. I was generally a pretty nice guy, and maybe I hadn't been so nice to her at lunch.

A few times I set my shovel against the fence and, using the pretense of taking a break, I walked through the orchard to see if she was on the lawn playing croquet or practicing her putting skills. But nothing was going on there. Later, I walked as far as the shed and peeked through the opening in the oleander hedge to see if she was lying poolside. But she wasn't there either. Once I walked all the way to the parking lot, figuring that if I ran into anyone, I'd make an excuse like I was getting a bottle of water from my truck. In reality, I just wanted to see if Bettina's truck was around, but it wasn't parked near mine anymore and the garage doors were closed so I couldn't look inside.

I don't know what would've happened if I'd actually found her. I'd been thinking I'd try out another apology, only this time I'd say it like I really meant it. But I never got the chance to see how that would work because she wasn't around. And then it was time to go home.

*　*　*

By the time I got home, I was tired to the bone. It's an expression people use, but I understood exactly what it meant that night. Literally the only thing on me that still felt solid was my skeleton, and there wasn't a muscle in my body that wasn't completely spent. If our house were burning down, I doubt seriously I could've gotten out of bed to save my life. Del and Claude kept coming in my room to bother me after dinner, but I barely had the energy to yell at them. After a while, they left me alone, I guess because it's not much fun messing with a dead guy and that's what I must have seemed like to them. I think Del was worried about me, but I heard Maman tell him I was okay, and I'd just had a long day and needed to sleep. Then she shut my light and closed the door softly and I knew I wasn't going to make it to the shower even though I needed one badly.

I couldn't fall asleep straightaway because something was poking around in my brain and it didn't want to leave me alone. At first, I was too tired to figure out what it was, but I knew I had to make my peace with it or I'd be awake the entire night. So I chased it round and round in my head, like a hamster on one of those exercise wheels that was never going to stop. And then, when I was about to give up, get out of bed, and go take a shower, the wheel stopped and the thing that was bothering me fell out like a dead rat.

Bettina told me the kids at school had turned her into a beast. When I questioned her about it, she'd said it was because maybe she was one. I hadn't even brought it up at lunch—I never even asked about it. And that was probably something I should've done.

After that, I don't even remember falling asleep.

* * *

I woke up at three in the morning with the room spinning around me, my head pounding, and my mouth feeling like I'd eaten glue instead of chicken for dinner. I sat up and swung my legs over the side of the bed and stumbled into the bathroom. When I took a leak, barely anything came out, and what did come out was orange. I didn't have to be a genius or even a doctor to figure out I was dehydrated. I went into the kitchen and drank glass after glass of water from the tap. I tried to think of how much I'd had to drink that day but the best I could come up with was the Arnold Palmer—even that I remembered gulping down like there was no tomorrow. I sat in the dark on the sofa staring at the square, actually trapezoid, of moonlight that beamed through the window onto the floor by my feet. After about twenty minutes, I felt almost normal, so I went back to the bathroom and took an extra-long shower even though we weren't supposed to waste water because of the drought. The hot water pulsing on the sore muscles of my back felt therapeutic. It also gave me a chance to think things over.

I'd completed two full days and one half day of my total obligation. I only had two fulls left and three halves. To-morrow was Sunday—church day. Last Sunday, Mr. Diaz told me not to come until one o'clock. But that was when I didn't know what I was supposed to do. Now I knew I had to trench the entire perimeter of the fence. It was much cooler in the morning and if I worked then, it would leave me with a free Sunday afternoon. I was already feeling somewhat rested and I still had another three hours to catch up on my sleep. I decided to set my alarm for seven o'clock so I could go in early.

Did Bettina have anything to do with my decision? Maybe. But at the time I didn't allow myself to admit it.

TWENTY-EIGHT

I won't lie and say it wasn't nerve-wracking ringing the doorbell of that delivery entrance, just like I had the week before, only this time it was worse. I waited a long time for someone to answer because it seemed to take these folks ages to respond to a doorbell ring. At my house you could make it to the front door in ten seconds flat no matter what room you were coming from, but the Diaz family had a lot more territory to cover. With that in mind, I rang a second time and waited about five minutes before giving up.

As soon as I got to the side gate I realized something was up. I knew the exact spot where I'd left off the day before, but the trenching line had been extended by maybe about twenty yards. Off in the distance, a lone figure toiled—slight and fashionably unfashionable in her "work clothes." There was Bettina bizarrely in the act of unloading a shovelful of earth onto the edge of the trench. And just at that moment, I was surprised by a feeling so unfamiliar I had to dig deep to place it somewhere in the catalog of my life

KATHRYN BERLA

experiences. It wasn't that dopey, stars-in-my-eyes feeling I got when I was around Masie, or even when I thought about her. It was more that same feeling of being a kid on Christmas morning when you first see all the presents under the tree. I could barely believe it myself but I was happy to see her.

If she saw me, I couldn't tell because she kept digging with a fierceness I was sure I didn't have when I was doing the same job. I walked toward her until I was close enough to see the gloves on her hands, the pink Converse sneakers and cap, the ripped jeans and the white T-shirt that looked pretty dirty and sweaty from where I stood.

"Oh," she said when I got close enough. "Didn't see you come in."

She leaned the shovel against the fence and drew the back of her arm against her forehead. Sweat looked good on her.

"You have some dirt where you just wiped," I said, and she took another swipe at it. "Now you have more."

She narrowed her eyes at me and for the first time it didn't make me flinch.

"Just messing with you," I said. "You don't have any dirt on you."

"I've done twenty-eight yards since you left yesterday," she announced.

"Twenty-eight, is it? Really quite impressive. You actually measured twenty-eight yards?"

"Yes, I did," she said, and I could see one of those steel measuring tapes clipped to the waistband of her jeans.

"Man oh man, are you going to be sore tonight," I said. "So, why'd you do it?"

"Do what?"

"Those twenty-eight yards."

"Because it needed to be done, obviously. I didn't think you'd be here until this afternoon."

I felt the devil sneak up inside me. "Are you sure about that?" I said. "After all, I was here last Sunday morning."

"And last Sunday morning you didn't know you weren't supposed to be here." She picked up the shovel and punched it into the ground.

"Give me that shovel." I put my hand lightly on hers. "It's my job, not yours."

"It's mine, too," she said without looking at me, and I did notice she didn't push my hand away or try to shake it off. And I didn't hurry to remove my hand from hers either, although this all happened in a matter of seconds, not minutes. She plunged the shovel again and that's when I noticed how taut and strong her muscle was under that soft, smooth skin. And that's also when I removed my hand.

"Seriously, why're you doing this?" I asked. "Even if I wasn't going to be here this morning, you knew I'd be coming in the afternoon. You should've left it for me."

"And I told you . . . it needed to be done. Do you think I don't know how to work after spending my entire life on this ranch? Do you think you invented work?"

"No, I didn't say that. It's obvious you know how to work. I'm just wondering why you'd want to, that's all. I mean, considering there are other people around to do the work for you."

"There wasn't anyone around this morning." She was still leaning on the shovel looking at me, and I was still standing there with my hands in my pockets, arguing with her like a fool.

"Well, now I'm around, so I can do it. Give me the shovel, please." I was pretty proud of myself, maintaining my cool and being so mature.

"No."

I lowered my voice and spoke slowly and deliberately, carefully enunciating each syllable. "I need the shovel so I can mark off my hours. I cannot mark off my hours if I'm not doing anything."

"Fine," she said and thrust the shovel into my hands. Then she marched through the orchard toward the lawn.

"Wait," I called out after her. "Are you coming back?"

Aargh! This girl is maddening.

Several minutes later, she was back with a different shovel.

"Where'd you get that?" I asked stupidly. I knew the answer.

"From the shed."

"It's not a trenching shovel."

"It will still work."

"Here, take this one and I'll use yours." I extended the handle to her, but she ignored me.

"I'm fine with this one."

She set to work about ten feet away from me. "Carlos told me there's probably a rattlesnake den around here, and one of the guys almost stepped on one in the vineyard yesterday."

"So it's good we're doing this," I said with a grunt as I hit a buried rock with the tip of my shovel. I started working my way around the rock, chipping at the edges so I could pop it out like a loose tooth. "Do you speak Spanish?"

"No," she said. "Just the little I've learned in school."

"How do you speak to Carlos, then?"

"He speaks English." She stood on the upper edge of the shovel blade and bounced a few times. The soil was tougher in this area than where I'd worked the day before.

"I didn't know that. He never spoke English to me."

"Maybe he doesn't like you," she said very matter-of-factly, the way you'd tell someone their fly was unzipped.

I could've followed through with something witty and biting. In fact, I was just itching to do that, but she hadn't really said it in a mean way. Besides, I didn't want to be cruel to Bettina. Hadn't I set my alarm for seven o'clock to have some alone time with her that morning? *Hadn't I?*

"How about your dad?" I asked instead. "Does he speak Spanish?"

"More like Spanglish, but better than me. He was born here."

"Nana Diaz?" I realized my mistake of being overly familiar as soon as I said it, but she didn't seem to care.

"She's fluent," she said. "Anything else you need to know about my life?"

What I really wanted to do—needed to do—was apologize for being such a thoughtless jerk the day before. I'd told her she didn't have a filter and then I'd proceeded to throw away my filter and say some hurtful things. If I was to be totally honest, I'd say it might be payback for my enforced month of labor. But Bettina didn't want me to be there and she'd told her dad to let me go. It wasn't her fault he was so determined to teach me responsibility and character, as if I didn't already have them. Bettina was odd—that much was true. But it's also true there were things about her I absolutely admired.

"Did you do the dishes this morning?" I said instead. "We wouldn't want your nana to get mad when she comes home from church." I mentally kicked myself in the butt and then pulled myself together to start over. "Bettina . . ." I stuck my shovel into the ground, holding it with my arm parallel to the ground like I was some sort of frontiersman staking a claim. I hoped that my confident-looking stance would give me the necessary confidence to apologize in a real way. "There's something I have to say to you."

"I know," she said, all the while digging. "And I accept your apology."

"What apology?"

"You were just going to apologize about yesterday, weren't you? So, I accept your apology."

This was the second time it seemed she had access to my thoughts—like somehow she'd stolen the password to my brain. I muttered something unintelligible. She was a thought hacker.

"And that's the second time you've said my name," she said.

"No, it can't be."

"It is."

I was still in the ridiculous position of holding the shovel upright with my outstretched arm.

"Yesterday, at lunch—I must have said it a dozen times."

"You didn't. Not once."

This had the effect of flustering me and I returned to my work. She was digging fast, keeping the edges straight and the depth consistent, which was hard, especially considering she had the bad shovel. But I was starting to catch up to her.

"How many times have *you* said *my* name?" It occurred to me it might have shot a bolt of lightning through me to hear my name come out of those lips.

"None."

"Ah-ha! That's what I thought."

"Ah-ha, what? This isn't a name-saying competition. I was just stating a fact. Just like you state a lot of facts and make a lot of observations."

That pretty much shut me down.

"Anyway," she said. "What *is* your name? Just B-O?"

"No, it's B-E-A-U. It's French. It actually means handsome in French." I waited for the compliment I hoped would follow.

"Mine's Italian," she said.

"Are you guys Italian?" I asked even though I knew the name Diaz wasn't Italian.

"I'm half Italian," she said. "My mom's Italian. My dad's side of the family is from Mexico."

"Interesting." I dug the last scoop of earth before catching up to her. "Where's your mom?"

"In Italy."

I immediately regretted asking. Italy was pretty far away so this couldn't be a happy story and maybe Bettina preferred not to get into it.

"That makes sense," I mumbled idiotically. "If she's Italian, she'd be in Italy."

"No, it doesn't." She waved me past her and I leapfrogged ahead about ten feet, so we could still hear each other. "It doesn't make any sense at all, actually."

"So, then why's she in Italy?"

"Because she left us . . . or rather, she left me."

"Why would you say that?" I turned to look at her, but she kept digging so I resumed my digging. "People don't leave kids. Their marriages just bust up sometimes."

"That's what Dad wants me to believe. He says she left because she couldn't stand the sight of him, but I know that's not true. It was me she couldn't stand the sight of. He's just trying to make me feel better because he loves me."

"It could totally be true. And if that's what he said, then why wouldn't you believe him?"

"You've met my dad. How could you not love him? Everyone loves him."

I thought about how I was only there working my butt off on the weekends because of her dad, and I thought maybe not everyone loved him so much.

"And besides," she said. "I overheard Nana talking to Dad about it, so that's how I know."

TWENTY-NINE

"I'm tired," Bettina said. "I need to sit down."

I could tell it cost her to say that because she wasn't the type to admit to a weakness. I knew that just from the short time I'd spent with her.

"Sit down," I said. "I was hella sore last night. Dehydrated, too . . . in fact, I was even a little sick."

She leaned her shovel against the fence.

"Why don't you keep me company?" I suggested. "It makes it go by faster when you have someone to talk to."

"Tell me about it." She looked around and settled about five feet behind me against a slender fruit tree and the meager shade it provided. "Do you like persimmons?"

"My mom makes persimmon pudding, but I can't stand the texture of the fruit: so slimy, way too sweet, and I hate the way it leaves a film on your teeth."

"Have you ever had a Fuyu persimmon? They're not like that, they're more like apples."

"A persimmon that tastes like an apple? I don't believe it."

"Try this." She stood and selected a beautiful orange fruit from the tree and tossed it to me. It was hard and had the shape of a tomato. "It's a Japanese persimmon . . . Fuyu," she said. She examined a few others before picking one for herself. She sat down again, leaning against the trunk, and took a bite.

"Is it okay?" I asked cautiously. "Eating it like this? Without washing it?"

"Haha! I wouldn't have thought you'd be the type to be scared of germs." She took another enormous bite and I could hear the crunching from where I stood.

"I'm not scared of germs," I said, rubbing the persimmon vigorously against my shirt and considering for the first time that she probably hadn't rinsed the grapes we had the other day. My mom washed every piece of fruit that came into our house and was always warning us to do the same. "I'm just not a huge fan of getting salmonella or whatever."

"Salmonella? Go wash it under the hose if you're scared." She took another big bite and crunched away. Two more bites and even the core was gone. She tossed the little bit remaining, barely a stem.

I wasn't one to walk away from a challenge, not that she'd actually issued one. What was the worst thing possibly alive on that persimmon? It hadn't been on the ground, but a bird could still drop a turd on it. I gave it one last rub against my T-shirt, then sank my teeth into it. It was delicious. Better than an apple.

"Good, huh?" She didn't rub it in or even remark on all my frantic T-shirt scrubbing.

"Yup." Crunch, crunch. "What did you hear your nana say?"

"Huh?"

"That day you heard your nana talking about your mom. What was she saying?"

"Oh, that." She took a deep breath and exhaled loudly like she was trying to get rid of the memory. "I was a bad baby, I know that much. That's what Nana said."

"How can a baby be bad?"

"I cried, like . . . all the time for a year. I guess that would be enough to drive anyone away. It would probably drive me away."

I looked at her sitting under that tree, her legs folded across each other. She was strong and determined. "I don't think so," I said.

"Well, anyway. My mom left when I was three, so I mainly just remember her from the pictures we still have. And then Nana had to leave the town in Arizona where she'd spent most of her life. All her friends. The house where she raised my dad and his brother. Where my grandfather, Papá Lupe, died. She had to come help my dad raise me, so who wouldn't be mad about that? I can understand why she'd hold it against me."

"That's all just speculation. You said you overheard her saying something to your dad."

I was done with my persimmon, having eaten it almost to the stem. I tossed what was left over the fence.

"When I was about ten, my dad hosted a big wedding reception for one of my second cousins. There were tons of people, maybe hundreds. And there was a huge line for food at the buffet table. I'd been standing in line for a long time, and right when it was my turn to serve myself, one of the guests, a woman I didn't know, cut in front of me and took a plate and started serving herself."

"And?"

"And I said, 'Excuse me but there's a line and I've been waiting for a long time and you just cut in front of me.' Then she turned around like she just noticed me and the huge line for the first time and she said, 'You're a very rude little girl, no wonder your mother left you. Weren't you taught to be respectful of your elders? Someone should give you a good spanking.'"

"Wow!" It was pretty hard for me to say more than that. How someone could be that cruel, I couldn't comprehend.

"Nana was walking by just at that moment and she heard what the lady said so she pulled me aside and I explained everything. I could tell Nana was mad at me, even though she didn't say anything, and she even went and got me a plate of food. But later that night, I heard her talking to my dad in his study. They thought I was already asleep in my room, but I was still awake and had come down to get a drink. Nana was saying I'd always been trouble and I should have shown more respect to the old lady. I could tell she'd been crying, probably because she got stuck with me after my mom left. My dad was really mad and said the lady, who turned out to be some distant relative, was never welcome in our house again. But yeah, that's when I learned the real reason my mom left us. Left *me*."

I walked over to where she was sitting and sat down beside her—not too close but close enough. "Listen," I said. "Sometimes old people get cranky. I don't know why— maybe it sucks to get old. But nobody ever left a baby 'cause they were bad. No *kid* is ever bad. Your mom had issues and who knows what they were? Maybe they were her own issues or maybe stuff between her and your dad. But it wasn't you, trust me. I know that much, and I don't even know you."

She shrugged her shoulders and stood up. "It's obvious that Nana agreed with the lady."

"I don't think it's obvious at all. Have you ever considered that maybe she was mad at the lady and not you? Or maybe even mad at herself for not saying something?" It bothered me that Bettina was so willing to believe the worst about herself. "Let me ask you something if it isn't too personal," I said. "If your mom's in Italy, and you're not really close to your nana, do you have anyone you can talk to? I mean, the way a girl talks to her mother."

Angie and Maman were always having talks about things. Me and Papa, too. I wanted it badly for Bettina—someone she could confide in like a mom.

"Ray's wife, Diane, is pretty nice. She talks to me when she's around."

"I guess that's better than nothing," I said, realizing it might not have come out the way I intended.

"Come on. We'd better get back to work."

But the rest of the time she gave up on digging. I knew she'd reached her limit with all the work she'd already done, and she'd proved her point. Whatever her point was, at least she'd proved it to herself, I could tell. But she stayed down there with me the whole time I was working, and whenever I advanced about ten feet or so, she'd pick herself up and move with me.

THIRTY

I'd been working about three hours under the hot sun when Bettina suggested taking a break.

"I don't think I should," I said. "I'm still on the clock."

"Who's going to know? Look how much you've done—*we've* done. There's something I want to show you."

I wasn't hard to convince even though I knew enough to keep my eye on the time and be back at trenching by noon.

"Where to?" I asked as she led me through the side gate.

"Follow me. It's a surprise."

I hoped it wasn't going to be another fancy luncheon she'd prepared but she wasn't heading toward the house, she was heading toward the vineyard where the tractor was parked.

"Hop on," she said after scrambling into the driver's seat. "I'll take you for a ride."

"You know how to drive this thing?"

"Of course I do. It's easy."

I was skeptical but intrigued. I hopped up and took the seat beside her. She fired up the engine and we took off, bouncing and jostling toward the avocado grove.

"I'll give you a tour," she said, "of the entire Diaz Ranch."

*　*　*

It was an enormous property, even bigger than I'd imagined after working there for two weekends. Acre after acre of beautiful unspoiled central California landscape. The most interesting part for me was driving through the avocado grove, though. The single avocado that brought me to the Diaz Ranch in the first place was just one tiny grain of sand in a sea of the green fruit. And that's another thing— the avocado is a fruit, not a vegetable, according to Bettina. Sure, it tastes and looks like a vegetable but it's technically a berry, so there you have it. Full cycle from the grapes, which are also berries, to the source of my favorite snack, guacamole, another berry.

Bettina was loaded with information about avocados.

"In some parts of the world, they're called alligator pears," she said. "Because they're shaped like a pear and the skin looks like an alligator."

And later on . . .

"Do you know they're loaded with fat? But it's the healthy kind of fat so it's guilt-free."

Her face lit up when she talked about avocados in a way I hadn't seen before. "We grow two kinds," she explained as we bumped our way between two rows of trees. "Hass and Fuerte. Which do you like best?"

I shrugged. "The kind my mom brings back from the supermarket." I honestly didn't know there was more than one kind.

"Most people like the Hass because that's the one the stores usually carry. But my favorite is the Fuerte."

"What's the difference?"

"There's a huge difference." She pulled the tractor up close to a tree and put it in park. She stood on the driver's seat and reached up to pluck a large bright green avocado. "Take it home and let it ripen for a few days," she said. "Then you can try it and let me know what you think. The skin is a lot thinner than the Hass so scoop it out gently with a spoon. Or peel it with a fruit peeler and eat it with a fork."

"I can't wait to try it," I said. "Although I usually like mine mashed and smothered in salsa."

"Just taste it before you do that," she said. "It's like heaven—so smooth and buttery. Nana uses them for baking cakes. Even making chocolate mousse."

I examined the avocado in the sunlight. It was a thing of beauty, really. Nature's perfect masterpiece, so simple and yet so tasty. Bettina put the tractor in gear and we chugged away.

"*Fuerte* means strong in Spanish," she continued. "That's how this variety got its name, because it can withstand freezing temperatures."

"It's hard to get used to that whole berry thing—first the grapes and now the avocados."

"Technically a persimmon is a berry, too," she said.

"I knew it! I *knew* you were going to say that. Just please don't tell me a hamburger is a berry or you're going to ruin my entire day."

And then an incredible thing happened. She laughed. Bettina Diaz laughed, and I was the one who made her laugh. I wasn't so conceited to think I was the only one or the first one to ever make her laugh. But I was the only one to make her laugh in my presence since I'd known her.

"Okay, I won't," she said. "I wouldn't want to burst your bubble."

I looked at my watch and realized how close it was to noon. "We'd better get back," I said. "Your dad will be home soon."

"I know." And she sounded a little wistful. Maybe even a little sad. "You know what I think about sometimes when I'm walking alone in this grove?"

"I have a feeling it's not guacamole."

"It's not. I don't even like guacamole," she said. "But seriously . . . I think about how amazing it is that the fruit won't ripen as long as it's on the tree. If you left it on the tree forever, it would never get ripe. I think that's how people are. They have to leave home in order to grow up, and that makes me sad because I love this place and I don't ever want to leave it."

And I could see how bad it made her feel just saying it. "You can always come back," I said. "After you've done whatever growing up you need to do."

She tucked a loose strand of hair behind her ear. "I will. I could never stay away for long."

By then we'd arrived at the spot where Ray kept the tractor parked. She turned off the ignition and we climbed out.

"Thanks for the tour. It was really great, and I had a nice time," I said. "I learned a lot, too."

And then I remembered the question I wanted to ask her, and it felt like such bad timing. It didn't seem like the right moment and it didn't seem like the right question, but I'd promised myself and I didn't want another night of tossing and turning because I neglected to ask. We were almost to the side gate, but I hadn't heard any cars driving across the gravel yet. No car doors slamming or garage doors opening. No voices other than our own.

"Last time we were talking," I said. "Right before the lunch. You said something about how the kids at school turned you into a beast. And when I asked why . . ." I glanced over at her and had the strange sensation she was drifting away from me like a helium balloon floating up into the sky. "When I asked why," I forced myself on, trying to grab at that balloon string to pull her back to me, "you said it was because maybe you *are* a beast. I know that's not true, so what did you mean?"

We'd arrived at the side gate and I opened it and paused to let her enter first.

"Beau, remember how this morning you asked if I did the dishes? Well, I didn't, and if I don't do them right now before Nana gets back, she's going to have a fit."

And she took off down the granite stepping-stones like Bambi, disappearing into a maze of persimmon, apricot, and cherry trees smothered at their roots by that insane colorful riot of flowers. I remember thinking then how people answer the question they wish they'd been asked instead of the question they're actually asked. And I remember standing there counting how many days it would be until I returned to the Diaz Ranch. And the last thing I remember thinking was . . . *that it was the first time she ever called me by my name.*

THIRTY-ONE

Weekdays and weekends were like living in two different worlds. In one sense, it's always like that. For Maman, weekends meant not going to work unless Khalil's parents were out of town. For Papa, it meant having people around instead of lying on the couch by himself all day. But ever since I started working at the Diaz Ranch, it felt like two completely different people occupied my brain depending on the day of the week. Pre-Diaz weekends consisted of hanging with friends, playing with the twins, doing chores for Maman and Papa, catching up on homework, and, most recently, hanging out at home while Angie and Maman went on and on about the wedding. Post-Diaz weekends consisted of hard manual labor. And Bettina.

Monday morning was a ride-my-bike day instead of a pick-up-Khalil day, and I was grateful for that. I didn't know how I was going to refuse Masie if she asked to go along now that she and Khalil were technically friends. With Ethan out of the picture and Khalil's almost certain offer to treat us at the diner, I figured even picking him up from school would be an attractive option for her. We kids from Bridgegate didn't get over to the Castlegate area very often, so it could almost qualify as a semi-adventure.

Another thing I dreaded was seeing Bettina at Castlegate with or without Masie in the seat next to me. Maman said I could drive her car on the days I needed to get Khalil. It was easier to maneuver through the school parking lot than the truck, used a lot less gas, and—I was hoping—would disguise me from Bettina in case our paths should cross. She wouldn't be looking for Maman's car, at least I hoped not. I hoped she wouldn't remember it from the accident, but I doubted it—there were thousands of cars that looked just like Maman's on the road, but the truck was one-of-a-kind.

That morning, after locking up my bike and catching up with my friend Ned in the parking lot, I practically wasn't surprised when Masie came into my field of vision, traveling in the same direction toward our lockers. I practically wasn't surprised that she was walking with Ethan the Goose—or at least he was walking and she was rolling along beside him on her skateboard. And I practically wasn't surprised they were holding hands and taking turns nuzzling each other's necks.

To be honest, I did register a moment of disappointment—I don't know whether it was disappointment in Masie or the general situation—but it didn't take me long to recover and I felt no outrage toward either one of them. Maybe they belonged together, I thought. Although Masie had limped through the past week using the crutch Krissy and I provided about her being too good for Ethan, clearly she didn't need it. Or believe it. And maybe Ethan wasn't such a goose, after all. Or maybe he was a Canadian goose, and those were considered somewhat handsome in the avian world. And who said a Canadian goose and a Persian cat couldn't coexist? After all, someone had written a love poem about an owl and a pussycat and how different could that be? So by the time I got to my locker, I was already talked down from the ledge and ready to carry on as Masie's friend. You could never have too many friends, after all.

"How was your weekend, Beau?" Masie asked at our lockers after Ethan dropped her off. Apparently, she didn't remember what I was doing with my weekends lately. "Did you have fun?"

"It was fine."

"Guess what?"

I didn't have to guess. I knew what was coming, but I was going to make her work a *little* for it. I wasn't just going to hand it to her on a silver platter.

"What?"

"Ethan and I are back together."

"*Really?* Wow. No kidding. Good for you."

"Yeah, I mean, I didn't expect it, but he called Friday night and asked if we could talk and . . . well, you know. One thing led to another."

Yeah, I knew.

She slipped her skateboard into her locker in a move I knew pretty well by then, slammed the door, and spun the dial.

"I'm happy for you, Mase," I said and realized I kind of was. "If you're happy."

"I am. So, hey, are you still going to pick up Khalil? Maybe I can go with you and we could hang out sometime."

But I found the idea to be not very appealing after the last time.

"I'm not really picking him up anymore," I lied.

"I still want to help with Angie's wedding. I can do flower arrangements and table settings, you know. I'm not letting Ethan take over my life like he did last time. This time I set boundaries, so I get some *me* time and don't neglect my friends."

"I'll mention it to Maman, but I don't think we'll have flowers." I hoped I didn't sound too under-enthused, but I realized at that point she was more interested in girl-crushing on Angie than boy-crushing on me. That was fine. I'd already accepted my non-relevance in her life in just the short amount of time it took me to cross the parking lot. But it didn't mean I had to love it just yet. And she wasn't the only one who could set boundaries and demand *me* time. "Anyway, I'd better get going . . . don't want to be late for chem."

"Okay, Beau. Tell your mom and dad hi from me. I love your family. They're so adorable and nice."

And Masie really was a good girl. A sweet girl. A beautiful girl. A girl any guy would be proud to have as a girlfriend. But she just wasn't interested in me. Not only did Ethan's reappearance in her life deliver that message loud and clear, but I couldn't think of one instance when Masie asked a question about me and then listened intently like she really wanted to hear the answer. She never took me somewhere to see something I hadn't seen before. She never helped me do something I didn't want to do that wasn't any fun. And to be fair, I never did any of those things for her, either.

I didn't blame her for any of that. She probably did all that stuff with and for Ethan. But she wasn't into me and that was okay. I thought I knew someone who was. And what's more . . . that day, I thought I knew someone I was into as well.

THIRTY-TWO

"Beau, my man!" Khalil slid into the passenger side of Maman's car. "Long time, no see, brah."

"It's only been five days, Khalil. Quick, get in and shut the door."

"Why?" The cool disappeared from his smile. "What's going on?"

"I just wanna get out of here before we get caught up in traffic."

The truth was I wanted to get out of there before I saw Bettina. It wasn't that I was afraid of seeing her like before. It was just that I didn't know how she'd react if she saw me at her school, and memories of our last encounter there still haunted me. We'd progressed to a new level in the video game of life, and I didn't want to start all over again at Level One.

"And before you say it, don't tell me to chill out," I added for good measure as I pulled into the through traffic lane.

"I want everyone to see you, that's the whole point," Khalil said, and then turned around like he half-expected to find Masie hiding in the back seat. "Where is she?"

"If by *she*, you mean Masie . . . she has a new boyfriend. Or an old one who's back in the picture."

Khalil unwrapped a Jolly Rancher and offered it to me.

"Oh, hey, sorry about that, man. I know what a bummer it is to get your heart squeezed like that. Been there."

I wondered if Khalil really had been there, but who knows. It is possible to have your heart broken without the other person even realizing you exist—I knew that much.

"We were never together," I said. "She's just a friend."

"For real?" Khalil squealed. "If I'd known that, I'd have put the moves on her. Then maybe she wouldn't be back with the old boyfriend."

"I guess anything's possible, lover boy," I said. "Anyway, she liked you . . . your company . . . as a friend."

I was clear of the school by then so there was no chance of a close encounter with Bettina.

"Guess what happened in school today? You'll never guess," Khalil said. He was transitioning back to the real Khalil as we moved farther away from Castlegate.

"I give up."

"No, guess. You gotta guess."

Khalil unwrapped another Jolly Rancher. He'd accumulated a pile of empty wrappers in his lap just since we'd left school. Personally, it took me a good ten, fifteen minutes to finish even one, so I wasn't sure how he did it.

"Okay, space aliens invaded your cafeteria."

"No, seriously. C'mon, guess again."

He rolled his window down even though I had the air conditioner blasting.

"I give up. How the hell am I supposed to know what happened at your school when I can barely keep up with what's going on at mine?"

"The Beast. She came up to me today after lunch."

He looked over at me with a huge grin. I felt my skin prickle just underneath the surface. I felt a hot rage, but I did my best to tamp it down.

"Please don't call her that, Khalil. It's not very nice."

"She's The Beast, Beau. *The Beast!*"

"Why do you say that?"

We were nearly at Khalil's house by then and I wanted to finish the conversation before I got him home. The last thing I needed was Maman listening in and then cross-examining me about Bettina Diaz. I pulled over to the side of the road in front of some random mansion.

"It's not just me. *Everyone* calls her that," he said.

"Okay, well, you're not everyone. Not in my car. Not if you want me to keep picking you up. Or you can go back to having L-Mom pick you up five days a week."

One of the police cars that patrols Khalil's neighborhood passed by going in the opposite direction. The car slowed and then stopped. It reversed until it was even with us and the cop stared out his window at me.

"Hello, Officer Yamaguchi." Khalil leaned over and waved out my window.

"Hey there, Khalil, didn't see you. How ya doing?" He waved and drove off.

We were alone again except for a guy mowing the lawn who stared every time he passed us.

"Why are you like that, man?" Khalil said. "What's up with you and Bett Diaz?"

The air smelled fresh, like summer. It was that mowed grass smell we didn't get too much of in California because of the drought. At least not in my neighborhood.

"Nothing's up. But since you were so anxious to tell me what happened, why don't you finish. She came up to you and then what?"

"She asked me if I knew that I'd made her trip and drop all her books that day. And if I knew I broke her sandal." Khalil laughed nervously. "Like that happened a month ago. I don't know why she's bringing it up now."

"And what did you tell her?"

"I told her, *no*."

"*Did* you know?"

"Yeah, but—"

"Then why didn't you say so?"

"It creeped me out when she asked me out of the blue like that. Like what's she going to do after all this time—sue me or something?"

"Khalil. When it happened . . . did you help her pick up her books or apologize for tripping her?"

"No, but—"

"Why not?"

"All my friends were there, and everyone was laughing. I was kind of . . . the hero, you know. She's The Beast."

"You know what, Khalil? That sucks."

He looked down at his lap and I could see he was twisting his hands together the way Claude does when he's anxious.

"I know," he said at last.

"So, what're you going to do about it?"

"I don't know."

I took a deep breath and raked all ten fingers through my hair. Maybe I looked like someone whose head was about to explode.

"Do you want to be a freshman jackass your entire life or do you want to be a man?" I asked as coolly as I could.

"I'm not going to be a freshman jackass my entire life because next year I'll be a sophomore," Khalil said, and I knew by the sound of his voice he felt bad and was paying attention.

"Just do the right thing, Khalil. Okay?"

"Okay," he said.

THIRTY-THREE

After that, there was another streak of the notorious Le-Francois bad luck. The next day when Maman went to pick up Khalil from school, he claimed he wasn't feeling well and he thought he might've gotten food poisoning from the meat loaf he had for lunch. They say actions speak louder than words—well, it wasn't too long after he got home that his actions started speaking a whole lot louder than his words. His parents were out of town, but his dad was supposed to be back early that night. Later on, his dad called and said the flight was cancelled because of bad weather and he couldn't make it home until the following afternoon. Naturally, Maman wasn't going to leave Khalil alone in that condition, so she brought him to our house with a bucket on his lap. We moved Papa to the bedroom and Khalil took the couch. Needless to say, none of us got much sleep that night.

By the next afternoon, it was obvious Khalil didn't have food poisoning but most likely some version of the stomach flu. The way we knew this was because everyone in the house had it by then, including me. Khalil was back on his feet and feeling pretty perky so that was the good news; whatever it was only lasted twenty-four miserable hours. Khalil refused to let his dad come pick him up. He said he'd made us all sick, so he was going to stay and take care of us until we were all better. Which he did really admirably. Trust me, it's not easy to take care of a 6'2" Cajun man who can't get himself to the bathroom at a moment's notice. Khalil earned massive bonus points in all of our books that day; in fact, Claude and Del regarded him as something just one step down from superhero status. And I realized what a fool I'd been to think Khalil would judge the way we lived.

The one bright spot of that day was when Khalil brought me a cup of ice chips and whispered that he'd managed to do the right thing before he came home sick from school. I didn't have the energy or presence of mind to ask him what that meant.

No sooner were we all back on our feet the following day when Angie called to say Jason had lost his job as a rep for an air conditioner manufacturer. We'd been hopeful for this one, which he'd actually held on to for six months. It wasn't Jason's fault, Angie explained; the company was going through hard times. Jason wasn't exactly a LeFrancois, thereby allowing him to piggyback on to our bad luck, but Papa allowed as to how he was close enough, which explained his inability to hold on to a job. The fact that Maman or Papa had never lost a job didn't change the way Papa saw it. He loved Jason—Papa loved everyone—and so it was simply a matter of the LeFrancois bad luck, and nothing could be done about it.

* * *

In spite of all this, or maybe because of it, the days passed quickly. A shake-up of your routine, even if it's bad—*especially* if it's bad—speeds up time, so it was already Saturday morning and my alarm was jolting me awake at seven o'clock. This time I didn't linger in bed and drag myself through breakfast and a shower. This time I had wings on my feet, and even the truck seemed to have them when, before I knew it, I was already at the turnoff to the Diaz Ranch. Imagine my surprise (and okay, maybe even delight) when I saw Bettina perched on the fence post like a little owl, apparently waiting . . . for me? I pulled into the driveway and stopped. She climbed into the cab beside me.

"I've been waiting," she said, clicking on her phone to look at the time, "for fifteen minutes."

"I'm not late. In fact, I'm exactly on time."

"I know that." She looked over at me. "I was early."

"Well, anyway, we're both here now so what's up? How've you been?"

I made the slow crawl down the long, narrow gravel lane.

"I can't wait for you to see something," she said, and it was only then I noticed her hands, covered with bandages, and her arms, crisscrossed by scratches.

"You look like you've been fighting dragons," I said.

"Oh, these?" She held her hands up in front of her, fingers outstretched. "Just a few blisters."

* * *

Ray and some of the other guys, including Carlos, were still in the parking area, shedding their jackets, rummaging for lunch buckets, generally getting ready for a long day of work. What I didn't want was to make the grand entrance with Bettina. That would only confirm their teasing from my first day at the Ranch. I hadn't even known her that day, and here I was, just a short while later, pulling my truck into the parking lot with Bettina sitting by my side. She seemed completely unfazed and even unaware of my apprehension.

She jumped out of the truck before I'd come to a complete stop and ran to catch up with Ray, who was walking toward the area where the tractor was parked. While I parked and prepared for *my* day, I could see her talking to Ray. When they were done, he looked over at me and waved.

"What was that all about?" I asked when she was back.

"I just wanted to make sure everything was good to go."

"Good to go where?"

"Follow me," she said.

I knew by then that Bettina loved surprises. I followed her through the side gate that led to the area where I'd left off working on the snake fence and was shocked to see the entire perimeter had been completely trenched. Bales of mesh wire dotted the inside of the fence about every fifteen to twenty feet.

"The digging's all done!" I said. "That's cool." It was the digging that was so mindless and backbreaking.

Bettina stood there proudly surveying the scene, hands on hips. She was wearing her faded ripped jeans (which now looked like real faded ripped jeans, not the kind you buy that way on purpose), an actual old white T-shirt (maybe her dad's?), and boots similar to the type Ray and Carlos wore. Her hair was pulled back into a ponytail and she was wearing the baseball cap with the white cat head. She had on aviator-type sunglasses with lenses light enough I could still see her eyes.

"I did it," she said.

"You? You did this whole thing?"

"Yep."

"Nobody helped you?"

"I told you, I did it myself."

She held up her hands as proof in case I doubted her, which I didn't.

"You know what, Bettina? You're kind of amazing," I said.

"You know what, Beau? I know." She smiled. "Just kidding. I know I'm not."

"No, you are . . . for real. I can't always figure you out, but I do know for a fact you're amazing."

She beamed bright as the sun.

"I had Ray put out the wire mesh for us," she said. Somehow, somewhere along the way, this had become *our* job, not mine. Fine with me. Odd, but fine with me. "With both of us working, it'll go faster."

"Let's get started, then," I said.

We began at the gate, which is where I'd left off.

THIRTY-FOUR

"Remember how we did this? We each take an end and lay it down in the hole. Then we fill it back up and pack the earth around it."

"And cinch the ties," she said. "I know."

I unrolled the first bale of wire, and we each picked up opposite ends the way people do when they're folding a sheet.

"On the count of three, we drop it in," I said. "One . . ." *Pause.* "Two . . ." *Pause.* "Three . . ." *Deep breath.* "Are you ever going to tell me why some kids call you The Beast?" I asked, hoping the mindless task of laying out the mesh wire would make it easier to talk about. It was something she'd brought up and then dropped. I felt it was something we needed to get out of the way, so we could move forward. I also had an idea it was something she needed to deal with before she could move forward with anything.

She narrowed her eyes and pressed her lips together. Her glossy eyebrows dipped toward the disapproving frown line right above her nose.

"Your friend said something to me at school, as if you didn't know."

"Who? Khalil?"

"As if you didn't know," she repeated.

"What did he say?"

We took up our shovels and began scooping dirt into the trench.

"As if you don't know."

"Bettina, please just tell me what he said, because, honestly, I don't know. Yes, I know he talked to you but when he told me about it I was in the middle of a gut explosion . . . a series of them, in fact."

"A gut explosion? That sounds mildly disgusting."

"Everyone in my family was sick last week and Khalil took care of us. At some point between when I was emptying out my stomach and emptying out my you-know-what, he told me he talked to you. Forgive me if I didn't express an interest in following up."

"Okay." She held up her hands in the surrender position. "Sorry, I had no idea you were sick and I'm glad you're better but please spare me the gory details. I happen to have a very strong gag reflex, and maybe . . ." She covered her mouth with her hand. "In fact, I think I might be coming down with it right now."

"Then spill the beans or I'll tell all. And, by the way, the incubation period is longer than fifteen minutes, I'm quite sure."

"Spill the beans?" She groaned. "Bad choice of words."

I was starting to think she'd go to any length to avoid the subject of her school nickname. I could've let it go and maybe I should've. But somehow, I had the feeling she needed to talk about it with someone. Maybe even with me. And finding out what happened between Khalil and her was the first step.

"Are we ever going to talk about it?" I asked as gently as I could. "Or do you really want me to drop it, because I will if you do."

We'd finished filling in the trench, so we started tamping down the earth with our feet like we were stomping grapes or something.

"He said, *sorry*," Bettina said.

"Just like that? I mean, nothing leading up to it?"

"Yeah, just like that. Almost as if . . . his *mother* told him to do it."

"What does it matter who told him to do it if he did it?"

"I guess it doesn't. But I know it was you."

We continued stomping around and not exactly looking at each other.

"This is like that square dancing we did in fifth grade," I finally said to break the ice. "Maybe we should link elbows and spin around." I laughed weakly because it wasn't really funny. She didn't laugh at all.

"We were spared square dancing," she said. "In fact, I'm not even sure what it is."

"Square dancing? Really? It's just this sort of . . . ah, never mind if you don't know. It's not like you missed out on anything. Let's start cinching and meet in the middle." I squatted down since sitting wasn't a position I enjoyed, not being limber enough to sit cross-legged. "Two ties per post, every other post."

"I know," she said.

"Do you have a pair of cutting shears to trim the edge of the ties, so it looks really nice?"

"No."

"Here, take these. Heads up, okay?" I tossed the shears to her. "Give 'em back when you're done."

"Your whole family was sick?" she asked.

"Yup. It wasn't pleasant."

"Do you have brothers or sisters?"

"Two brothers and a sister, but only the boys live at home. My sister's already out of the house."

"And both your parents?"

"Yup."

"It must be nice to have siblings. And both parents."

I had to think about that. "It is, I guess. There are ups and downs."

I looked over and saw she was perfectly posed like the Buddha. Straight back, legs folded, long slender fingers nimbly securing the ties.

"Your mom probably hates me, right?" She snipped off the end of a tie, then scooted to the next post.

"I'll answer your question if you answer mine."

"What question?"

"You know what question." It was an ugly thing that would have been easier to drop, but I made a decision not to do the easy thing. Bettina didn't seem like a girl who would normally choose the easy way. I knew from personal experience that she confronted things head-on. A ladybug crawled up my arm. I let it walk onto my hand, and when it reached the tip of my finger I pointed it toward Bettina, so she could see. She leaned forward and watched it fly away.

"Ladybug, ladybug, fly away home. Your house is on fire. Your children are gone," she said. Even though I'd heard that rhyme before, I hadn't really given it much thought. Right then, it seemed especially sad.

"That's somewhat depressing," I said.

"I know."

"Do you still want to know if my mom hates you?"

She reached into the bag for another tie. "Are you sure you really want me to answer your question? You think the ladybug poem is depressing. Well, so is *my* poem."

"Try me." I scooted closer to where she was working.

"Go back to where you were," she said. "I don't want to look at you when I tell you."

I scooted back, sat down, and started cinching another tie. "Okay, I'm not looking."

"I didn't always go to Castlegate," she said. "I used to go to private school, but I begged my dad to let me go to CG because I wouldn't have to wear a uniform and you've probably noticed I like fashion."

"I've noticed you do a lot of wardrobe changes," I said, my gaze aimed firmly at the fence in front of me.

"So last year my dad finally let me transfer after a whole year of begging."

"Weren't you going to miss your friends?" I asked. "Wasn't it intimidating to start a new school?"

"Why would it be?" She seemed genuinely puzzled.

"I don't know. I guess it would be for me, that's all."

"Why's that?" she asked, and I thought sometimes she could be so unbelievably obtuse, but I kept my voice level so she wouldn't think I was trying to get the last word in.

"I mean . . . I'd miss my friends, I suppose."

"Oh that," she said. "I've never had a ton of friends, so that wasn't an issue. I don't even want a lot of friends. If I need company, I hang out with my cousins. School's just . . . *school*. It's where you go to learn, right?"

"Okay, I guess so," I said. Technically, she was right, but school was more than that to me.

"And the trade-off of being able to wear whatever I want was worth it," she added.

I have to be honest, carrying on a conversation when you can't look at the other person is not only uncomfortable, it's just plain weird. Nevertheless . . . her rules. So, proceed.

"The first week, I was invited to a party by two girls I met in one of my classes. They seemed nice. Even though I don't like parties . . . *at all* . . . I wanted them to like me since I was new, so I agreed to go. The night of the party, I wanted to cancel but my dad pushed me to go. He worries about me not having enough fun or friends because his personality is totally opposite mine. He loves me, but he doesn't *get* me."

I wondered at that moment if *I* got Bettina. My personality was probably totally opposite hers, too, because I liked people and being around them as long as they're what Papa calls *good people*. So, could a person like me and a person like Bettina coexist? I figured we could if we both understood what the other needed and respected that. After all, if Masie could coexist with The Goose, then anything was possible.

"So, you went to the party," I said. "And then what?"

"Worst mistake of my life," she said, and I knew sometimes things can go south at a party, so I was a bit nervous for why it was the worst mistake of her life.

"The party was at this guy's house—Decker, a name I wish I could forget but probably never will. Anyway, he's gone now, graduated last year. And he was the star player on the baseball team, which apparently is one of the best teams in the state. I didn't know anything about that and wouldn't have cared if I did."

But I *did* know that. Papa and I followed local school sports and Decker's name always came up in the stats. I remembered him being out for his final season, but I just assumed he'd had an injury. And anyway, CG baseball wasn't *that* much on my radar, even though everyone knew they had a state championship team.

"I was a sophomore, new kid at school. He was a senior who was having a party at his house where I didn't even want to be. Dad dropped me off and I was getting a ride home with the girls who invited me, but they weren't there when I got to the party. Decker answered the door and seemed nice and attentive. I asked about my friends and he said they'd probably be there soon and he could show me around in the meantime."

I stopped cinching the ties. "This doesn't sound like it's going to end well," I said.

"And it didn't. I don't feel like going into the details because I've already done that with people I feel a whole lot less comfortable around than you. But basically, at some point, I wound up alone in a room with him and he took that as a green light to shove me down on the sofa and forcibly make out with me. I told him to stop, and tried to push him off, but he wouldn't stop. When he yanked my dress up, I bit his lip so hard I tasted his blood in my mouth. And then while he was screaming and calling me a bitch, I ran out of the room. By then, the girls who invited me were there, and when I finally found them, they asked what happened and were super-supportive. The mom of one of them came to pick us up and we waited out front on the street, so we wouldn't have to see Decker."

"And then?"

"And then I went home, Dad was furious, we went to see the principal the next day, and Decker got suspended from school and wasn't allowed to play his last season of baseball. He also had to do mandatory counseling after he finally admitted the truth."

That explains his absence, I thought. *But not why Bettina got turned into The Beast.*

"Dad wanted me to transfer back to my old school, but I refused. I didn't want Decker to win and I was grateful to the school for what they did, considering that at first it was his word against mine, and I was a new student. But everyone started treating me like a pariah afterward . . . even the two girls who invited me to the party. They were so supportive until it came to Decker not being able to play his last season. And Castlegate didn't take home the championship like they would've if he'd been there . . . at least that's what everyone said."

"Ah, crap, that sucks," I said, and I glanced over at her. She'd stopped working and was staring at her gloved hands.

"Don't look at me," she said. "I told you . . . not until I'm finished."

"Are you finished?" I asked.

"Yeah."

"Well then . . ." I scooted over right next to her. "Well then, I'm really sorry that happened to you." I put my thick leather gloved hand over her thick leather gloved hand and left it there for a second. "I'm glad you shared that with me . . . that is, if it helped you."

I wasn't a great one with words, but I wanted to let her know she had a friend if she wanted one.

"It does, thanks," she nodded. "I wanted you to know, really. You can probably guess the rest . . . my general social awkwardness, my way of speaking my mind even when people don't want to hear it, the fact that I'm generally an in-trovert, and all the rumors spinning out of control . . . that's why people like your friend, Khalil, call me *The Beast*."

"Hey, he won't be doing that anymore," I said quickly. "I can guarantee you he's seen the light."

"So you talked to him about me before I even told you the real story? You did that for me?"

It was the first time I'd ever heard her sound unsure of herself. In a way, it was refreshing to know she was just like the rest of us with regular people insecurities, but the reason behind it was too sad. It didn't make me feel good at all. In fact, it made me feel pretty bad just then.

"I always knew you were good people," I said. "I can always tell. I have a sense for it."

"You missed a tie," she said.

"So did you."

She looked back to where she'd been working. "You're absolutely right."

"I know."

The sun felt hot against the back of my neck. Our shadows leaned against the fence and then spilled through to the other side. A light breeze ruffled the hair that had fallen out of her ponytail.

"Bettina, I wish everyone knew who the *real* beast was, but you'd never get back the peace of mind he stole from you, and it wouldn't make up for your pain."

"I know that," she said. "It's alright, and I don't need to be comforted. I'm fine and I'm strong."

She was definitely strong. But at that moment, reliving that time, maybe not so much.

"You do realize that once you get out of high school, you'll most likely never see those kids again and then *you* get to decide where you want to be and who you want to be around . . . people who appreciate someone brave enough to tell the truth like you did."

"That's like forever—before I graduate from high school."

"No, it's not. It'll go by fast as long as you keep your eye on the prize."

"What's the prize?"

"What you want from life. What you *expect* from life. And not to ever settle for anything less than that. So, for whatever it's worth, count me as an *actual* friend."

A smile barely lifted the corners of her mouth, and if I wasn't sitting so close, I would've missed it altogether. But as quickly as it came, it disappeared like a mouse poking its head out of a hole to take a look around.

"So, does she still hate me? Your mom?"

I clipped the end of the tie and leaned over to hand her the cutting shears.

"Of course not. She never did hate you. She was mad at you, but my folks could never stay mad at anyone for very long."

THIRTY-FIVE

Sunday morning marked the beginning of the end of my third weekend of work. After that day, there was only one last weekend with Bettina. I looked forward to being able to call my time my own again. I looked forward to paying off our family's debt and I was proud I was making that happen. I was also proud I was helping to make Bettina's world a little safer in the process. The snake fence, something I'd never heard about before I started working on it, would be a barrier between man and beast. There was nothing I could do about the "men" who turned Bettina into a beast, but at least my forced labor was helping her world in a small way.

Besides that, I was becoming used to her company. Maybe even a little more than that—maybe even a little excited about the prospect of her company as I drove to the Diaz Ranch that morning.

My heart felt happy when I saw her waiting for me, perched on the fence post where the street met the gravel lane. I say my heart felt happy because that's exactly where I felt it. Not in my nerves and veins like when I hit a home run in Little League in the sixth grade. Not in my head like when I got a test back in English I thought I was going to flunk and instead saw B+ and a smiley face on the top right corner. When I saw Bettina, I felt it in my heart. A kind of flopping feeling like there might be a dying fish stuck inside my rib cage, followed by a spreading warmth the way you get when you slap on one of those muscle-pain relief pads.

There hadn't been any talk between us on Saturday about when I'd be arriving the next day. I think we both knew without a doubt that I'd come in the morning when it would just be me and her and nothing else but that big old Diaz Ranch, with all its avocados and grapes and rattlesnakes and everything else. And when I say I saw her perched on the fence post, the image of an owl came to mind again, with her wise dark eyes that widened when she was interested in what you were saying and narrowed when she was shutting out the world or something she didn't like about it. I'd seen her as Bambi, too, scampering through the flower gardens, so there was that, but I'd given up trying to categorize Bettina. There was no neat and tidy spirit animal for her. She was complicated and mysterious. She was full of surprises.

* * *

When she got in the truck, she was quieter than usual, so I asked what was up.

"I got in trouble today," she said. "With Nana."

"For what? Not doing the dishes again?"

"Dad and Nana are going to a barbecue at my second cousin's house this afternoon, and Nana wanted me to go with them. To church and then the barbecue afterward."

"You should have gone," I said, thinking how disappointed I would've been if I'd been there on my own the whole time without Bettina. "Why didn't you?"

"I didn't want to," she said. "We have to . . . finish the snake fence before you leave. It's too important."

This would've been the part where I said something to her about how I didn't necessarily have to leave forever. That maybe we could continue to see each other outside of my work obligation. And that's what I wanted to say but I didn't have the nerve to say it just yet, and I figured I had one more week to work up to it. Then I *would* say it. How she'd react was out of my control, but at least if I saved it for the last day and she turned me down cold—at least then I wouldn't have to face her and feel her pity or scorn or my own humiliation. There was no telling with Bettina how it would go. She was different.

"We'll finish it before I leave," I said instead. "If we work really hard."

"And that's what I want to do." She nodded in agreement. "Work really hard and get it done. I told Nana and she said that's why we pay people to work on the Ranch and started in on my dad about spoiling me."

"I don't get how you wanting to work translates to your dad spoiling you."

"I know, right? But Nana thinks I should make more of an effort to be social, and working on the fence is just an excuse not to be."

"How about your dad? What did he say?"

I asked cautiously, because technically her nana was right. If Bettina and I didn't finish the snake fence, someone else would do it better and faster. But it was our thing, the cause that bonded us together. It was the place where we shared stories and secrets, hers too dark to tell in any other way.

"Dad loves me to the moon and back, so he does everything he can to make me happy. I don't think he's ever really understood me, but nobody does." She glanced over at me shyly. "He doesn't care that he doesn't understand me, though. He loves me anyway."

I pulled the truck under the massive tree and an acorn landed on the roof of the cab, making a clattering noise, much louder than its size warranted.

"Anyway, I like being out here on the Ranch. It's better than going to a dumb barbecue with a bunch of people."

"But you love your fashion—all your clothes and shoes and sunglasses. All your outfits. I'd have thought you'd want to go places to show them off. To show off how good you look," I said and then literally bit my tongue, sensing right away I was saying something dumb.

"Can't I just do that for me? I mean, I do like fashion but not for other people. I like it for myself."

"Yeah, and I didn't even mean that. Not sure why I said it."

"Did I ever tell you my mother's a fashion designer in Milan?" she asked.

"You never mentioned it. Do you want to be a fashion designer?"

"Oh, hell no," she said. "I want to be a rancher like my dad. Let's get to work."

Bettina and I had the job down. Muscle memory kicked in, so we didn't have to think about what we were doing anymore. We'd become an efficient team without even thinking about it, but it was slow-going, detailed work. Not having to communicate about the work left plenty of time for talking.

"Is your family excited about your sister's wedding?" she asked when we were laying down another length of mesh wire.

I had to stop and think for a minute. I didn't remember telling Bettina about the wedding.

"You told me that's why you pick Khalil up from school," she said, as if she could read my thoughts or at least the puzzled look on my face. "To give your mom more time to prepare for the wedding . . . remember?"

I hadn't remembered but then I did. This girl listened. She heard. And she remembered. I wasn't sure if anyone outside my family had ever listened to me that carefully before. Paid that much attention.

"Of course, I remember," I lied.

"So, are they? Excited, that is."

"I don't think my little brothers care too much except maybe they pick up on everyone else's excitement. And I'm not that involved, even though I offered to be the photographer. But my mom and dad, yeah. Totally. Obviously, Angie is, too."

"You'd make a good photographer," she said. "I can see it in the way you pay attention to detail. The way you work and appreciate everything around you. I could see it that day I showed you the avocado grove."

"Thanks." No one had ever given me that particular compliment, and my services as a photographer weren't exactly in demand. It got me to thinking that maybe I could be a good photographer and I made a mental note to start taking some more artsy shots. "By the way, that avocado was amazing," I said. "And I'm not going to be the photographer because everyone agreed Angie should hire a professional. Makes sense, I guess. What if I screwed up and they didn't have pictures to show their grandchildren?"

"Where's the wedding venue?" she asked.

Venue sounded like a too fancy way of describing it. "It's like a rec building at a park near where we live. They rent it out for functions. And if the weather's nice, there are picnic tables right outside."

"That sounds nice," she said. "Music?"

"A friend of Jason's is deejaying. They're trying to save money because of the cake and the . . . venue, and the photographer. The food, too, even though my mom's making most of it. And my mom's making Angie's dress and her own dress and the two bridesmaid dresses. They're skipping the flowers." I'd heard these details so many times they bored me, but Bettina seemed interested. "Jason lost his job and money's kinda tight," I added.

"Oh," Bettina said, and I wondered if it was a struggle for her to imagine what life would be like if money was tight.

* * *

Two hours into it and our shoulders and backs were killing us from hunching over the wire mesh, tying it to the fence posts.

"Time to get out the wiggles?" I looked up and grinned at Bettina.

"Get out the wiggles? *Really?*"

"Yeah, why not?" I tried not to sound too hurt. "If it's good enough for preschool Beau, it's good enough for high-school Beau."

"What do you suggest?" Bettina stood. "I don't know about wiggles, but my shoulders and neck are feeling it."

"Race you to the lawn," I said. "But you have to stay on the footpath. I'll give you a head start."

"Please! I'll give *you* a head start," she said.

And we took off, me starting first and expecting to win. But Bettina overtook me, even somehow leaping past me while never leaving the granite stepping-stones. We threaded our way along the meandering path, which wound through the entire orchard, scampering through the flowers just like Bambi and . . . Thumper. Bettina made one final leap that landed her on the grassy lawn.

"Can I interest you in a game of croquet?" she asked once I caught up.

"Nope. My policy is to only lose at one event per day," I said.

I was panting and laughing from the exertion. I stopped to catch my breath but she was off again, across the lawn, disappearing through the gap in the oleander hedge. I followed her onto the pool deck, which was the first time I'd been there since that first day.

"Cannonball!" she yelled and executed a perfect one, clothes and all—right into the pool.

I looked around. No one there but us. I cannonballed in right behind her.

"Oh well, I needed a new watch," I said when I came up for air. "Forgot about that."

"And I needed new boots." It was only then I realized she was wearing her big clunky leather work boots.

I looked up and blinked at the bright cloudless sky. The sudden cool of the water against my sore muscles felt good. For about one second. And then . . .

"I should get back to work." I dragged myself and about a hundred pounds of wet clothes to the side of the pool where the steps were. "Oh, man, this is going to feel so shitty. Why did I follow you in?"

She slogged up behind me, dragging her own hundred pounds, maybe two hundred considering the boots.

"Because you really wanted to do it," she said. "Or you wouldn't have. We'll be dry in an hour."

We got out and sat by the side of the pool for a few minutes letting the sun work its magic on our backs. Our clothes felt heavy and clammy—nothing worse than wet jeans, not to mention wet shoes and socks. I wanted to take my shirt off, but it seemed inappropriate.

"Why were you so weird that first day we met?" I asked.

She didn't have to think about it too long and she didn't get mad at the question either.

"I don't like a lot of people," she said. "I don't necessarily trust them at first. I told you I'm a bit of an introvert, so people have to prove themselves to get into my life."

"An introvert without a filter."

"At least I'm not a know-it-all who always has to have the last word." But she looked over at me and smiled so I knew she was kidding around. "That day when you challenged me about the coffee I threw in the pool, and then you sang that stupid song. That's when I knew you were okay. You were different."

"Just okay?"

I pulled off a shoe and let the water drain from it, and then did the same with the other one. Then I took off my socks and squeezed them out the best I could.

"Maybe a little better than okay. Nice . . . you know. I liked being around you because you were real."

"Liked?"

I put my socks on while she took off her boots and repeated what I'd just done.

"Okay, *like*."

Her hair was completely out of the ponytail by then, swept back from her face revealing it more fully than I'd ever seen it without sunglasses, floppy hats, or hair to hide behind. It was a beautiful face, I decided, and was surprised I hadn't realized that before. Without the camouflage, without the backstory, it was open and trusting—round in shape, which made her seem younger than her age, dark satiny eyebrows and thick eyelashes glistening under the sun from moisture. I didn't know where our hats had gone until I saw them floating in the pool.

"I'll get them," I said. "I know where the net is. Be right back."

By the time I fished our hats out, Bettina's socks were wrung dry and her boots were back on.

"Can you please tell your mom I'm sorry for the way I acted?" she said. "I get embarrassed just thinking about it."

"Sure, I'll tell her," I said.

This would've been my second opportunity to tell her she could tell my mom herself when I brought her to my place to meet my family and see my part of the world. But again, I held back. Next Sunday. When I could disappear if she laughed in my face.

"I feel really bad you have to spend your weekends working here when your family is so busy getting ready for your sister's wedding," she said.

"Don't worry about it, okay? There's not much I can do now, and I'll be able to help out with the cooking and setup the week before."

She stood up and twisted her hair into a loop on the back of her head before stuffing it inside her cap.

"I'm ready," she said.

"Back to snake country?"

I held my wrist up to look at my watch and it was still running. Unwilling to rush the magic of the moment, we strolled across the lawn, retracing our steps along the footpath, side by side taking turns with who was on the stepping-stones and who was off. By the time we got back to where we'd left off work, we were about fifty percent dry.

*　　*　　*

The rest of the time went by too fast. I actually could've gone on for another couple hours and our progress was incredible. But around one o'clock we heard a cough behind us and we both turned to look.

"Dad," Bettina said, her voice slightly panicky. "Why're you home?"

I'd never seen Mr. Diaz looking soft and thoughtful the way he looked at that moment. The man I'd seen before was a guy in control. A guy who oozed the word *respect*, but also someone you wouldn't mess with.

"I dropped Nana off at the barbecue," he said, "but I wanted to come home and see how you were doing."

He gave me a look that seemed half interested and half suspicious, for which I couldn't really blame him. Who was I, after all? The hired help home alone with his precious daughter.

"Nice work," he said, and nodded at me in particular, as if he was giving me the signal it was time to clear out.

"I guess I'd better get going," I said, grateful we were both completely dry by then although we probably looked a mess to him. Hopefully, I thought, that could be explained away by sweat and hard work. "See you next week."

After that, it was a long and lonely drive back home.

THIRTY-SIX

I won't say my life came to a standstill during the school week because it still had its moments. There was still locker-time with Masie in the mornings, although that was becoming less and less interesting to me. There was still hanging out with my friends, which consisted of talking about girls, sports, and video games, although I was usually only half listening and not letting on anything about Bettina, which I wanted to keep private until I knew where I stood with her. There were still the days I picked up Khalil and, fortunately, I never ran into Bettina again. And there was still always lots of action around my house.

So, I won't say my life came to a standstill because life never does, even though plenty of times I'd like to pause and rewind it or pause and fast-forward. But I will say I was looking forward to the weekends a lot more than Monday and Friday and everything in between. I will say Bettina was in my thoughts even during the days I wasn't with her. And it wasn't like it had been with Masie, which was a hundred percent pure lust—not a bad thing, don't get me wrong, but nothing more than a thing. I realized I never really listened to Masie and she didn't really listen to me. And why should we, when our minds were both someplace else?

With Bettina, it was different. I'd spent time learning who she was and each hour we were together, we peeled off a few more of the layers everyone carries around for protection. And that was the exciting part, like a mystery novel you don't want to put down and you never want to end. That's what I was feeling for Bettina.

*　　*　　*

I had mixed feelings that last weekend—excitement about regaining my freedom, but anxiety about Bettina. Sunday, I'd find out how she felt about us—if she wanted to keep seeing me or if it was going to be bye-bye Beau. It's not like I was proposing marriage or anything, but it almost felt that nerve-wracking. In one more week, there'd be a real marriage and then my family would get back to normal and—just maybe, if things worked out—Bettina could come over and see for herself what *my* life was like.

"Where do you want to go to college?" she asked that last Saturday. We were so close to the end, rushing to finish in time.

"I'm not going to college," I said. "I've always loved building things and my dad knows someone who's a contractor. He doesn't have kids and he's getting older, so he's looking for an apprentice to help out. If I make a commitment to work with him for three years, he'll teach me everything he knows and even pay for my classes. And then who knows?"

"That's what you want to do?"

"Yep, that's what I want to do. Maybe a few years at junior college . . . get an AA. How about you?"

"Something to do with agriculture. I'm going to inherit the Ranch one day, so I need to know what I'm doing."

"That's a big responsibility."

"Not when you love it like I do."

I couldn't imagine what it would be like to love a place. I didn't love a place, only people. Only my family. But I could see how it would be possible to love the Diaz Ranch, especially if you'd spent your entire life there.

Even while we were talking, half of my brain was rehearsing the next day's scenario. We would finish up for the day and hopefully the snake fence would finally be done. I was pushing hard to make that happen, only taking fifteen minutes for lunch on Saturday over Bettina's objection. Then, when it was over, I'd ask Bettina if she wanted to take a drive, and that was something I was pretty sure she'd say yes to. There was a place not far from the Ranch, a trailhead where you could leave your car and hike into miles of open space. It was pretty there, and quiet—not quite a park but lots of trees and shade. I'd seen it on my way home and stopped to scope it out.

Hidden from Bettina behind the seat of the truck would be the picnic lunch I'd packed that morning. Even though I wouldn't have china plates, Arnold Palmers, chairs, cloth napkins, or a table, I'd spread out a red checkered cloth in the bed of my truck and I'd serve her lunch in *my* style.

When we were done, I'd take her home and casually ask if she wanted to hang out with me sometime.

That was my plan and I was going with it. Smooth? Maybe even Khalil could've come up with something better, but I couldn't so I hoped she'd like it.

* * *

In California where I live, sometimes the hottest days are the ones right before the weather turns cold—Indian summer, they call it, although I'm not sure why. This was one of those days: a heat so ferocious you knew it would expend itself by night, giving way to a shiver-inducing darkness; the air so still, it could annihilate any breeze dumb enough to take it on; and the quiet . . . that's what always got to me, the quiet that made you feel sad for something you were about to lose. That's the kind of day it was, and it hung heavy like the wet shirt I'd had on when I climbed out of the pool.

Bettina and I were together that day, but we were also apart.

"Even though you said last week she's not mad at me, I still feel bad," Bettina blurted out, "about your mother."

"I told you it's not a problem. She's fine. Not mad at all. Not furious, not even angry."

"I want to do something to make it up to her," Bettina said. The two of us had tied so many ties, I believed we could tie them in our sleep. We didn't have to look at what we were doing anymore, although that day I was fixated on them, more as a way to keep myself grounded. "I'd like to buy her something. What does she like?"

Wow. I have to admit that stopped me cold, it was such an alien concept to me. But then I reminded myself it wasn't Bettina's fault if she thought like that. She'd been isolated on this ranch with all her money for her entire life.

"You don't wanna do that, Bettina," I said as gently as possible. "That's not the way you get friends. And if you do get friends that way, they're the wrong kind."

She flushed rosy-red in her cheeks through the richness of her natural color, so I could tell my words were hard on her. I hadn't meant to embarrass her, but I didn't want Bettina to think my folks were something that they weren't.

"One day you can just make a nice gesture," I mumbled, not wanting to bring up the subject of hanging out just yet. After all, it wasn't quite time.

THIRTY-SEVEN

The average person would probably be bored hearing about that Sunday morning. Waking up an hour earlier than I usually did. Packing up napkins and paper plates. Slopping together a few sandwiches and throwing in some fruit for good measure. Filling a thermos with real lemonade instead of my usual water. Washing the only two matching plastic cups we owned. Scrounging around for a box of cookies the twins hadn't decimated. Even hosing the dust off the truck, which seemed to surprise my parents. Getting in the truck and realizing it was almost on empty. Driving two miles out of my way to get the cheap gas from the cheap gas station, and then having to turn around and go back home because I'd forgotten my wallet. That's just the normal type of stuff that happens to people who aren't even distracted and nervous. But arriving at the Diaz Ranch twenty-five minutes late and finding Bettina still perched on the post, still waiting for me like she knew all along I was just running late and would be there sooner or later . . . well, that was what made everything up to that point so worth it.

Driving down the long gravel lane with the tires crunching underneath us, I realized this would be the last time I made this trip involuntarily.

"You know what today is?" I asked, since Bettina hadn't said a word.

"It's your last day," she said. "I know."

"I was going to say it's the day we finish the snake fence."

"You think we'll make it? I'm not so sure."

I pulled up under the oak tree like I'd done seven times before and we got out. Bettina was definitely in a mood that day, and I was, too, but probably for a different reason. We trudged silently up to the gate and I opened it, waiting for her to go first the way Papa insisted even though some girls thought that was sexist. When I went through and closed the gate behind me, we stood for a minute and admired our work. It was clean and expertly done. I don't think Ray could've found an uneven spot or a tie that hadn't been clipped just right, a post that was untethered where it should've been. Not even if he went along every inch of the perimeter and took a whole day to check it out. We'd done a pretty perfect job. Now it was time to put a finishing move on it.

As if to reinforce the nervous uncertainty of that day, it was stifling hot and the sun wasn't about to give us a break, not even with one lousy cloud. Bettina stopped to wipe the sweat from her forehead with the back of her hand.

"You've got dirt on your face," I said, but she didn't fall for the trick that time.

"Now you've got more," she said instead.

"No filter."

"Always have to have the last word."

I glanced over at the work we'd done so far. The end was in sight—so close and yet so far.

"You know a little game I always play?" I asked. "I try to match up people with their spirit animals—like an animal they resemble physically or maybe just in their actions."

"So, what's my spirit animal?" she asked.

"That's the thing . . . I can never quite pin one down for you."

"Are there any candidates?"

"I have a few. An owl . . . a fawn. But neither one fits. You're just you."

"Remember, I'm The Beast," she said sullenly. "That's my spirit animal."

"Don't say that, Bettina. It bothers me to hear you say it."

"Why?"

"Because it's not true." I looked over at her, hoping she could read the meaning behind my eyes, that I was genuinely beginning to develop feelings for her.

"How can you be sure?" was all she said, and then we both went back to work.

* * *

A few hours passed without too much talking and I was ready for a water break. I kept my cooler in a shady spot close to the gate.

"Want me to grab a water bottle for you?" I asked. "I'm getting one for myself."

And just then I saw Mr. Diaz winding his way down the footpath toward where we were working.

"I didn't know your dad was home," I said. "Isn't he supposed to be at church?"

"Nana went with someone else," she said quietly. She didn't even look at me when she said it, like she couldn't bear to rip her attention from the tie she was cinching. "Dad said he wanted to keep me company today."

I thought it was strange she hadn't mentioned it. Bettina kept working without once looking up all the while I was waiting for Mr. Diaz to get to where we were.

"Good morning, Beau," Mr. Diaz said when he was near enough. "Or is it afternoon yet?"

"Good morning," I said and checked my watch. "It's technically three minutes into the afternoon."

"You two have done a fine job, a really fine job," he said. "You're almost done, aren't you?"

"Yes, sir," I said and wondered why Bettina wasn't saying anything, and why she wasn't looking at her dad.

"I'll tell you what," Mr. Diaz said. "Why don't you put away your things, Beau, then come around to the house to see me. Bettina, why don't you go get dressed, Honey, and I'll take you out to lunch." He turned and walked back up the path toward the house.

He was going to take her out to lunch? There went my plan for the surprise picnic. I was going to have to think fast to come up with Plan B. But whatever I came up with in the next few minutes was bound to be a disaster.

Bettina acted like she hadn't heard a word he said, and she kept working away like he hadn't even been there. Like

I wasn't even there. I pulled off my gloves and wiped my face with the sleeve of my shirt.

"What's wrong with you?" I asked. "Why didn't you say anything to your dad?"

"It's important," she said, "to finish the snake fence."

"Why do you think your dad wants to talk to me? It's not one o'clock yet."

She didn't answer.

"Bettina, you know that Ray or someone else will finish the fence if we don't."

And still she didn't answer.

"Hey, how do I get to the house?" I asked. "Back door, front door, delivery entrance?" I only half-joked.

"Go to the front door and ring the bell," was all she said.

"Okay, I'll be right back."

And then I walked out the gate and all the way around to the front door where I rang the bell for the first time since that day I came looking for a solution to Maman's car accident.

THIRTY-EIGHT

"Ah, Beau," Mr. Diaz said when he opened the door. "Come on in, son."

He stepped back, opening a path for me into the palatial ranch house I'd never seen from the inside before.

"Let's go to my office," he said.

I followed him through a huge rambling room with over-stuffed leather sofas and chairs that looked so soft and buttery it seemed you could melt into them and never have the energy or desire to get up again. A huge wall-mounted TV beamed a cool image of a green expanse of lawn with a white golf ball bouncing and then rolling smoothly, stopping inches from a hole. An immense aquarium was built into a stone wall where fish as colorful as the flowers in the orchard darted behind giant chunks of pink and green coral when we walked by. He led me into his office, the walls of which were lined with bookshelves filled with more books about agriculture and avocados and vineyards than I could take in all at once.

"Have a seat."

He motioned me to the red leather chair facing his enormous desk, and he took a seat in a chair behind the desk, which looked like it cost more than my family made in a month. He opened a drawer and rummaged through it until he came up with a pen, then he carefully pulled a single sheet of paper from the top of a stack to his right. All this time I was a little stunned into silence, trying to come up with a logical reason for what was happening. Mr. Diaz scribbled something on the sheet of paper and then pushed it toward me.

"Bettina wrote this," he said. "She does a lot of the paperwork for our business. Smart girl, that one." His pride couldn't be more obvious.

I glanced down at the form in front of me:

Today's Date:_____

Both parties agree that the work obligation has been completed and there is no further obligation on the part of either of the undersigned regarding the traffic incident on _____.

Signed:

Beau LeFrancois

Lupe Diaz

"Should I sign now?" I asked, and he nodded, sliding the pen toward me.

Once I signed, I passed the form back to him and he got up to use the copy machine on the shelf behind him. He handed me the original.

"It's yours to keep," he said.

I stood up, figuring our business was done and wanting to hurry to intercept Bettina before she came into the house. My picnic was a bust and I wasn't sure what I was going to do to salvage the day, but I knew I at least had to talk to her privately. Mr. Diaz stood and extended his hand across the desk, so I took it and we shook.

"I'll tell you what," he said. "I can see you're a fine young man and you've got a strong character." *Well, at least we got the issue of character settled*, I thought. "I can also see you might be a little sweet on my daughter, and that's fine by me as long as you treat her respectfully."

Whoa! I couldn't believe my ears. All my worrying about rejection—at least now I was in tight with Mr. Diaz. All I had to do was convince his daughter, and I hoped it wouldn't take too much convincing.

"Thank you, sir," I said, blushing furiously.

"I had a good feeling about you when I told Bettina I was going to release you from working after that first weekend. I didn't really want to punish you, but I was worked up about those darn kids coming onto our property and stealing avocados at night. I know it didn't have anything to do with you. And what happened with your mother and Bettina, well, that was just one of those unfortunate circumstances that could've happened to anyone."

We were both still standing, and I nodded, but what I heard didn't make any sense. He said he wanted to release me after the first weekend. And then what? I didn't have to wait long to get my answer.

"Bettina told me she called to tell you, but you said you weren't going to back down on an obligation that was rightfully yours. That you insisted on seeing it through to the end—I have to say I was impressed."

I felt myself being carried off in a tidal wave of blushing that was no longer from embarrassment. Instead, its source was fury and I realized I was flushing and not blushing. Bettina hadn't called me. We had never even exchanged numbers. It had never seemed appropriate to suggest it. This was an outright lie on her part, and it was at my expense.

"I've been keeping an eye on you since then and you were true to your word. Thanks again, son. You can get your things together and take off. Your obligation has been fulfilled."

I must have said "thank you, sir" or "thank you, Mr. Diaz" again before he walked me to the back where he opened the sliding door, so I could get to the orchard by crossing the pool area and the lawn. I must have said that, but I don't remember anything. Except I remember my heart pounding in my ears. I remember feeling totally betrayed and bewildered. I remember my legs carrying me along the now familiar path toward Bettina, legs that moved by rote but didn't feel a part of me.

And I remember the expression on Bettina's face. She knew, of course she knew. That's why she'd been quiet all day. That's why she'd asked me how I could be certain she wasn't really The Beast. And now I wasn't sure I could answer that question.

"What . . ." My lips moved, struggling for words to summarize and neutralize the betrayal and anger and confusion I was feeling at that moment. But the words didn't come easy. My emotions were outpacing any rational thoughts, if there were any left by that point. "What were you thinking?"

"Beau . . ." she said, before words failed, too.

"Do you think my life is a game? Do you think I'm a toy? Why weren't you just honest with me?"

"I'm sorry," she said pitifully. "I didn't want to lose you."

"Lose me? You can't lose something you don't own."

"I know, that's not what I meant," she said. "Please just let me explain."

I noticed she was still wearing her work gloves and she really did have a dirt smudge on her face. But it wouldn't have been funny to point that out to her. Not anymore.

"This ranch has always been my safe place," she said. "It's always saved me. But when I met you, I knew I didn't need the Ranch like I did before. I didn't need to hide, because a person could be a safe place, too. I was in a safe place when I was with you."

"I'm sorry, Bettina . . . I can take almost anything except lying. I can't take lying. If you'd just been honest with me, I might have stayed . . . I *would* have stayed. But it would've been *my* decision, not yours. You understand?"

And when she didn't say anything, I knew she did understand. And I knew she'd understand what I was going to do next.

I walked to the gate and picked up my cooler. Then I opened the gate one final time before latching it behind me. We hadn't finished building the snake fence. But we'd come so close.

THIRTY-NINE

By Monday, Masie was back in my life again. She and Ethan had split up over the weekend and this time she really believed what Krissy and I once told her about being too good for Ethan. Only I wasn't so sure I believed it anymore—Ethan had never wronged me in any way, nor anyone else I knew for that matter. And yet, it was nice to have the distraction of Masie's company at a time when I couldn't clear the gloomy cobwebs from my brain. With the wedding only a week away, all the better. Maman had invited Masie, and Masie hadn't forgotten.

"Mr. LeFrancois, I could paint that cast for you to dress it up a little for the wedding."

"Wha?" Papa was horrified. "No, I don' tink so."

Papa wasn't one to have anything to do with fanciful things like painting casts. But in the end, Masie worked her magic and convinced him to let her do it. She did a pretty realistic depiction of making it look like a black pant leg with a fancy black shoe at the end. Even Papa thought it looked cool, and the twins were spellbound watching Masie do her thing.

"Masie is Beau's girlfriend," I heard Claude whisper in a way-too-loud voice.

"No, she's not," said the ever-perceptive Del. "They don't make googly eyes at each other."

I know Masie heard because she kind of smirked. But at that point, I didn't care if she heard or not because Del was right. It wasn't true, and it never would be.

*　*　*

Friday night, Masie had a bunch of us sitting around the table making flowers from colored construction paper because we couldn't afford the real thing. We had three kinds of paper flowers: Masie's, which looked pretty good, although nothing like real flowers; mine, which looked something like tomatoes someone threw against the wall; and the twins' flowers, which looked like . . . well, not really like anything at all, but you could tell they'd once been construction paper.

At the same time I was making paper flowers, I was helping Maman out in the kitchen slicing vegetable sticks, keeping an eye on the pulled pork in the slow cooker, and stirring the jambalaya that Maman made under Papa's strict instructions and suspicious eye.

"No tomatoes," he'd holler out from time to time. Not that we had access to most of the other genuine ingredients his family cooked with back in Louisiana. The most important thing for him is that we didn't sneak in any tomatoes.

"Otherwise, it's Creole jambalaya," Maman whispered to Masie.

"And what's the difference?" Masie whispered back.

"I heard 'dat!" Papa hollered. "Big difference."

And then came the history lesson of the Acadians from what's now called Nova Scotia in Canada and how they got their butts kicked in the French and Indian War and basically had to get out of town, so they moved to Louisiana. *Les Acadians*—that's French for *the Acadians*—Cajun . . . get it? Anyway, the most important thing to remember, according to Papa, was "no tomatoes in the food."

While all this was going on, we heard a car drive up and I went to the door to see who it was. Angie was out with friends and Jason was home sleeping off his bachelor party, so I wasn't sure who was behind the wheel of the minivan. Leaving the rest of the family to monitor the cooking and paper-flower creations, I walked outside just as a woman was getting out of the van.

"By any chance, are you Beau?" she asked.

"Yep, that's me."

By then Maman had joined me and I could hear Papa calling out, "Who is it? Who's d'ere?"

"It's a van, Mr. LeFrancois," came Masie's soothing reply.

"I'm Diane Gooch," the lady said. "Ray's wife, from the Diaz Ranch."

I froze for a second and the look on Maman's face was one of extreme concern.

"Is everything alright?" she asked, probably waiting for some of that LeFrancois bad luck to rain down on us the night before Angie's wedding.

"I'm making a delivery," she said. "To Beau."

I could see two young girls through the windows of the van and they looked pretty excited. One of them was struggling to open the door from the inside. Diane turned around and beeped open the sliding side panel door with her remote key.

The girls hopped out of the car, their arms filled with bouquets of flowers—splashes of brilliant colors that exuded clouds of luscious scents that took me back to the days in the orchard. Diane leaned into the van and started hauling out more and more. Maman's arms were loaded and so were mine. And still there were more. By then Masie had come outside to help, and her eyes lit up like she'd been transported to the moon.

"These are amazing," she said. "They're sooo beautiful."

"We can't afford to pay," Maman said, her face already crumpling a little at the thought of losing all this beauty if it should come to that.

"It's a gift," Diane said, "for Angie. Picked and arranged by . . . *at* the Diaz Ranch."

She looked at me meaningfully like she had something else to say but was holding back. Maybe it was Maman and Masie being there . . . Claude and Del, too. There was no way I was going to send the flowers back and ruin everyone's day. But there was no way I was going to pump Diane for any information either. If the flowers were from Bettina, which I knew they were, then *she* should've brought them herself in that big new truck of hers. *She* should have the courage to come apologize in person. Not to send some flunky to do her dirty work.

"Thank you," I said, "for bringing them."

Diane gave me what I thought was one overly long last look before she said her goodbyes, leaving us with a houseful of the most awesome flowers Angie could ever dream of.

I truly believed I recognized every last one of them.

FORTY

(Happily Ever After?)

Who can help but enjoy themselves at a wedding? Even I was having fun. Masie and Khalil were the only ones of my peers there. Papa invited Khalil the day he nursed us all back to health after getting us all sick in the first place.

The flowers were a huge hit and they transformed that otherwise gray and generic public facility into a real venue where magic could happen. Angie looked beautiful, but she always did. That day, though, she looked even more beautiful with a smile that wouldn't quit. Even Jason looked okay in his rented tux. And he was actually pretty nice to me, even during the times there wasn't anyone else around to witness it.

Papa conducted the ceremony from his wheelchair. It was a good one, which he fortunately toned down at the end by leaving out the unlucky part of the LeFrancois legacy. He only mentioned the good part about how we were lucky in love. And he made sure to remind Angie that one never puts tomatoes in the jambalaya—just in case she should forget after a lifetime of being reminded.

After that, Papa danced with Masie, which consisted of a roll around the floor, with Masie more or less pushing his wheelchair. The most recent estimate from the doctor was another two weeks in the cast and then a whole lot of physical therapy. But slowly we were getting there.

Khalil danced with Masie more times than I could count. It was a good thing I wasn't jealous, and I also had a few dances with her myself. But in spite of the food and the flowers and the music and dancing and general happiness of the occasion, I still had a nagging, lingering sadness that wouldn't go away. Every once in a while, I had to push it down deep and then I was good to go again, for a while at least.

There wasn't any alcohol at the event, it being a public facility, but I don't think anyone missed it. We all felt drunk with happiness and with life by the time it started to get dark and the caretaker showed up to throw us all out. We pretty much had everything packed up and ready to cart out by then anyway.

Masie and Khalil and I were making trips back and forth to the truck, carrying all the stuff we brought that wasn't being thrown away. The night had already turned cool, but the room was hot from the sweating bodies and all the dancing and energy. It felt good to be outside. Khalil dumped a garbage bag full of whatnots into the back of the truck and then took his cell phone out of his pocket. The glow lit up his face, transforming it from a normal face to an *omigod* face as he stared at the screen.

"Whoa!" he said. "Beau, take a look at this."

"What is it?" I asked, but I honestly wasn't expecting to be amazed at anything Khalil had to share on his phone, unless the world had come to an end or something I didn't know about while we'd been busy partying. I wanted to finish up and go home. I was beat. Angie and Jason were long gone, and Maman already had Papa in the back seat of her car. The twins had left earlier with friends who were having them for a sleepover to give the rest of us a break after the monumental task of putting together a wedding. I'd already made a note to self—elopement when it was my turn to get married.

Khalil looked up from his phone. "It's Bett," he said. "She's blowing up on Instagram."

That got my attention and got me over to Khalil's side in about two seconds flat.

"I wanna see, too." Masie squeezed in between us.

I grabbed the phone from Khalil, which is something I'd never normally do, but patience and good manners were out of the picture just then. The look on my face must have kept Khalil from objecting.

I scrolled through the comments one by one.

Beast is bit, said the original post, an image of a big old rattlesnake's fangs dripping with venom. My gut clenched at that awful nickname and the thought of what might have happened. Bettina was bitten. By a rattlesnake. She was in the hospital if Instagram could be believed, and I, for one, was going to believe it unless and until I heard something different. I scrolled on.

Bett Diaz?	reply ♡
Yep	reply ♡
Haha!	reply ♡
That's cold-hearted. No one deserves to be bit by a snake	reply ♡
Not even another snake?	reply ♡

> She may be The Beast but she's still human last I checked   reply ♡
>> You checked? Lol   reply ♡

I honestly thought I was going to be sick. What kind of people were these? But I needed to know what happened to her, so I kept reading.

> Not me. I wouldn't dare get that close   reply ♡

And then the further I scrolled, a funny thing started to happen. The tone of the comments was changing before my eyes. Good people were finally chiming in. Good people were speaking out.

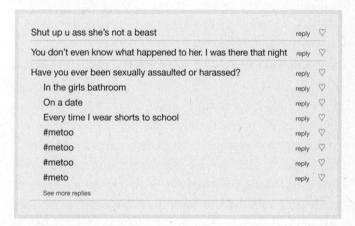

> Shut up u ass she's not a beast   reply ♡
> You don't even know what happened to her. I was there that night   reply ♡
> Have you ever been sexually assaulted or harassed?   reply ♡
>> In the girls bathroom   reply ♡
>> On a date   reply ♡
>> Every time I wear shorts to school   reply ♡
>> #metoo   reply ♡
>> #metoo   reply ♡
>> #metoo   reply ♡
>> #meto   reply ♡
>> See more replies

And then . . .

> Every one of us sucks because we all failed her   reply ♡

I took a few screenshots, texted them to myself, and pushed the phone back into Khalil's hands. "Let's go. If there's anything left here I'll come back for it tomorrow."

Masie and Khalil squeezed into the truck beside me without uttering a single word, but I could see Khalil bent over his phone catching up on what I'd just read.

It was only because the truck was so old that I didn't speed on the way to drop off first Masie and then Khalil. Because my foot was saying *go, go, go* but the truck was saying *shift first, shift second, shift third . . . groan.*

Nobody said much, or maybe they did but I wasn't hearing anything except the roar in my ears. At one point, Khalil mentioned a picture of the hospital someone posted along with the caption *Get well, Bett.*

When I dropped Masie off, she turned and took my face in both her hands, looking me right in the eye.

"This is so romantic, Beau. Like a fairy tale. Let me know how she's doing, okay?"

It didn't feel romantic. It just felt like I needed to be with Bettina.

I parked the truck at the hospital and ran to the information desk at the main entrance. The guy behind the counter warned me that visiting hours ended in ten minutes, so I'd have to hurry. He gave me Bettina's room number and it seemed like forever before the elevator doors opened. I jogged down the hall, slowing to a fast-walk when I saw someone in scrubs coming toward me. When I got to her room, the door was open. I could hear Mr. Diaz and see the back of Nana's gray head. And I heard Bettina's voice loud and clear, which was a huge relief. I knocked. Once. Twice. And then stepped inside.

"Well, Beau," Mr. Diaz said. "Good to see you, son."

I glanced at Bettina and her normally dark complexion looked pale green under the fluorescent lights. Her eyes were wide and dark and silent—full of secrets.

"I'll tell you what," Mr. Diaz said. "We'll leave you two alone since visiting hours are almost over. I'll see you tomorrow, Honey." He leaned over and kissed the top of her head. "Come on, Mother."

Nana Diaz was uncharacteristically quiet. She wasn't doing any of that hopping around like she usually did—the finch movements. She went to the head of Bettina's bed and smoothed her granddaughter's hair a few times with fingers crooked from age.

"We'll see you bright and early, Bettina dear," she said and smile-grimaced. I thought I detected moisture on her sharply jutting cheekbones.

It seemed clear that neither Mr. Diaz nor Nana Diaz had any idea what had gone down between Bettina and me on my last day at the Ranch. Once they left, I walked to the door and pushed it as closed as I thought would be acceptable in a hospital setting. Bettina was in a double room, but fortunately the second bed was empty.

"Why are you here?" she asked. "How did you know?"

"Khalil."

"How did he know?"

"He saw it on Instagram."

"Oh my God," she groaned. "My dad ran into the mom of a girl at my school. She's a nurse here. So, word travels fast, I guess."

"I guess."

What was wrong with me? I usually had no trouble talking to people, especially Bettina. But I was tongue-tied, as they say. So many thoughts were racing around my head. Had I failed her by not finishing the snake fence? Stupid thought, I know, but it occurred to me. Had I just failed her in general? As a friend?

"What happened?" I asked. "The flowers . . ."

"I wanted that for Angie," Bettina said. "You told me she couldn't afford flowers and I was thinking everyone should have flowers for their wedding and we have so many."

"Did you cut them yourself?" I knew at that moment she had.

"I planned it all out in advance . . . the arrangements. Which ones I would pick. I waited until Friday, so they wouldn't wilt, and I started right after I got home from school. I wanted them to be perfect for . . . Angie."

"And then?"

"I had everything picked. All of them arranged in vases. I was going to pack them up and deliver them to your house because I had your address from the day of the accident. But I thought of one more thing I wanted to add to the bouquets. It's this type of geranium that smells like peppermint. Do you remember it?"

I remembered the scent of peppermint from the first time I walked through the orchard. It came from a huge cluster of geraniums that seemed to spread like weeds. I'd passed it a hundred times, and each time I did, I always breathed deeply.

"I had my headphones on, and when I reached down to take some cuttings, it felt like a hot knife sliced through my hand. It was a baby snake . . . maybe a teenager, I don't know. Not too big, though, maybe just a foot or two."

"What happened then?"

"I screamed, and Dad heard me. Ray and some of the other guys, too. They all came running over and Dad looked like he was going to pass out. It was so scary to see him looking that way, but he picked me up and told me to stay calm and brought me to the emergency room."

"Why didn't Ray's wife tell me what happened?"

It killed me to know all that time Bettina was suffering in the hospital, I was home thinking mean thoughts about her. Dancing at the wedding.

"I made her swear she wouldn't. I asked Ray if Diane would deliver the flowers for me and promise not to say what happened."

"Why, Bettina? You're a crazy stubborn girl."

"I didn't want you to come to me out of guilt. I wanted you to give me a second chance because you heard me ask for it out of my own mouth. But not for this reason. I don't even know if you're here to give me a second chance now, or maybe you're just here because you feel sorry for me."

I thought about it for a second. I did feel sorry for her, of course. Who wouldn't? She looked so pale and small in that bed with the sheet pulled up almost to her neck. But that's not why I was there, was it?

"I haven't stopped thinking about you once since that last day I was at the Ranch," I said. "Not once. I would've come back to you. Maybe it would've taken me a month to come around to it, but I would've come back. This just sped up my feelings. Put everything in perspective."

"Do you forgive me?" Her eyes were wide and pleading.

The door opened, and a woman in a long white jacket walked in. Her tag said *S. Yelavich, MD*.

KATHRYN BERLA

"I'm Dr. Yelavich," she said. "Miss Diaz, how are you feeling?"

"Better now," Bettina said.

Dr. Yelavich looked at the monitors, picked up a chart at the foot of Bettina's bed, looked at that, and scribbled a few things down.

"You were an unlucky girl, weren't you?" she said. "About twenty-five percent of rattlesnake bites are what we call dry bites in which no venom is released. But you got a good dose of venom. The young ones tend to be less disciplined about releasing."

She pulled down the bedsheet, giving me my first glimpse of Bettina's arm. It was so swollen and red it looked like it might explode. I drew in a sharp breath and hoped Bettina didn't notice.

"The hand is where we usually see bites on humans for obvious reasons," Dr. Yelavich went on in that dry tone doctors have like nothing fazes them. "On dogs, it's the nose. Or so I've been told. Any racing heart, dizziness, nausea, metallic taste?"

"Not anymore," Bettina said.

"Okay, you're doing very well considering what you've been through. We're going to release you tomorrow and send you home with instructions. The main thing is to keep an eye on the swelling and call us if anything changes for the worse."

"I will."

The doctor looked over at me as though noticing me for the first time. "Visiting hours are over," she said. "The nurse will be by in a bit." And then she was gone.

Bettina and I looked at each other. I sure as hell didn't want to leave, but I could hear the nurse in the hallway and I knew she'd be coming in soon.

"So," Bettina said, "do you forgive me?"

"I forgive *you*," I said. "Do you forgive *me*?"

"For what?"

"For abandoning you. For not finishing the snake fence."

Bettina rolled her eyes. "Carlos finished the snake fence. The snake was probably there all along. Life's never a hundred percent safe, you know?"

"Can I see you tomorrow?"

"I guess I'll be home for a while, so you can see me whenever you want."

"When do *you* want?"

"Tomorrow. Today. Right now."

"When you're better, I want you to come meet my family, okay?"

"I'd like that," she said. "Really. A lot."

"These are screenshots from Instagram," I said, handing her my phone. "I wanted you to see what people are saying." I'd deleted the first post that called her The Beast. She didn't need to see that one.

Bettina scrolled through the images one by one, her expression never changing. "It isn't necessary for you to show me these," she said.

"I just . . ."

". . . thought it would make me feel better? I told you, it doesn't matter. I already know I did the right thing."

"Sorry, then."

I must have looked pretty pathetic because she handed me back my phone and looked up at me in that straightforward way of hers. "You know what?" she said. "It does make me feel better. It's going to make the school year a whole lot more pleasant."

"Bettina?"

"Yeah?"

"That last day . . . I'd planned a surprise lunch for us, but nothing went according to plan. I was going to ask if you wanted to keep seeing me. You know . . . hang out."

We heard the nurse talking to the patient in the next room. It seemed like she'd be in to check on Bettina next. Our time was running out.

"This would be the part where you kiss me." She tilted her head back, eyes closed, lips puckered, and I thought about the first time I'd seen her in that position at the side of the pool. That day, it had almost seemed like she'd been poised to kiss the sun. But it was me she wanted now. It was me she was finally asking for.

"There you go again," I said. "No filter. I was just about to do that."

It was one of those mysteries of life, the way opening your heart to a girl also opens your eyes to her beauty. But there she was, in a ratty old hospital gown, green under the fluorescent lights, and her afflicted arm resembling a fat pink sausage—but to me she looked just like Sleeping Beauty.

"And there *you* go—always having to have the last word."

She reached up, wrapped her good hand around the back of my head, and brought my face down to hers. And what resulted was a first kiss that wasn't bad at all. In fact, it was quite spectacular. That kiss told me everything I needed to know in just one moment of bliss.

First and foremost, it confirmed Bettina and I were now solidly together in happily-ever-after land.

Second, it proved Papa was wrong. The LeFrancois family wasn't unlucky in life but lucky in love. Because if you were lucky in love, you sure as hell were lucky in life.

And finally, it taught me something about the very nature of being alive—a pretty hefty accomplishment for just the pressing together of two sets of lips. What I learned during that kiss and all the moments leading up to it is a truth I'll never forget. There's a little bit of beast in every person. And in every beast, there's a human heart with a story of how it got to that place. A story waiting to be changed with understanding. A story waiting to be changed with just a kiss.

Acknowledgments

I'm so grateful to Amberjack Publishing for allowing Beau and Bett's story to be told. Cherrita Lee, we've been through a lot, and I consider you a great friend and keen observer of life and people. Dayna Anderson and Cassandra Farrin, thank you guys for your tireless efforts on my behalf.

One of the great perks of being an author has been the friendships I've made along the way—author friends who, like me, are always thinking about that next plot point or character weakness or just dreaming up a way to describe a sunset that's never been done before. There are too many of you to name but I'd like to mention a few who have been part of my daily (or at least weekly) life for years. Thank you, Agathe, Christy, Grace, Kristy, Lisa, Macy, Megan, Melissa, Suellen, Vera, and Vicky. Writing can be a lonely undertaking and your friendships have stood the test of time and have been such an enormous gift to me.

Dr. Sofie Y, thanks for being my emergency on-call physician. What would Bett have done without you?

To the Diaz family, you guys are an inspiration in every way.

To my darling and beloved family, thank you so much for everything you do to keep me happy and sane. I love you all: George, Jeremy, Lucas, Corey, Samantha, and Nishita Berla; and Hilary Helfrich.

And thank you to Greyson Berla for all the smiles and giggles.